My Friend Flicka
Part 1

My Friend Flicka
Part 1

Mary O'Hara

Dragon

Granada Publishing Limited
Published in 1966 by Dragon Books
Frogmore, St Albans, Herts AL2 2NF
Reprinted 1971, 1973, 1975

First published in Great Britain by
Eyre & Spottiswoode 1943
Reprinted fourteen times
Copyright Mary O'Hara 1943
Made and printed in Great Britain by
C. Nicholls & Company Ltd
The Philips Park Press, Manchester
Set in Intertype Plantin

Chapter One

High up on the long hill they called the Saddle Back, behind the ranch and the county road, the boy sat his horse, facing east, his eyes dazzled by the rising sun.

It seemed like a great personage come on a visit; appearing all of a sudden over the dark bank of clouds in the east, coming up over the edge of it smiling; bowing right and left; lighting up the whole world so that everything smiled back.

The snug, huddled roofs of the ranch house, way below him, began to be red instead of just dark; and the spidery arms of the windmill in the gorge glinted and twinkled. They were smiling back at the sun.

"Good morning, mister!" shouted Ken, swinging his arm in salute; and the brown mare he rode gave a wild leap.

To keep his seat, riding bareback as he was, he clapped his heels into her sides, and she leaped again, this time with her head down. Stiff-legged and with arched back she landed; and then bucked.

Once, twice, three times; and Ken was off, slung under her nose, hanging on to the reins.

She backed away and pulled to get free, braced like a dog tugging at a man's trouser leg.

"No you don't!" gasped Ken, sitting up to face her and clinging to the reins. "Not that time you didn't –"

She jerked her head viciously from side to side. Ken's teeth set in anger. "If you break another bridle –"

This thought made him crafty and his voice fell to a coaxing note. "Now Cigarette – be a good girl – thatsa baby – good girl –"

Responsive to the change of tone, one of her flattened ears came forward as if to peer at him and see if he spoke in good faith. Reassured, she stopped pulling and moved up a step.

Ken got warily to his feet and went to her head, still talking soothingly but with insulting words.

"Thatsa girl – stupid face – whoa, baby – jughead – no sense at all –" and this last was the worst possible insult on the Goose Bar Ranch where a horse without sense was a horse without a right to existence.

Cigarette was not wholly deceived but stood enjoying the stroking of Ken's hand and awaiting developments.

"D'you think I'd ever ride a ornery old plug like you if I had a horse of my own like Howard's?"

The frown faded from his face and his eyes took on a dreamy look. "If I had a colt –"

He had been saying that for a long time. Sometimes he said it in his sleep at night. It was the first thing he had thought when he got to the ranch three days ago. He said it or thought it every time he saw his brother riding High-boy. And when he looked at his father, the longing in his eyes was for that – for a colt of his own. "If I had a colt, I'd make it the most wonderful horse in the world. I'd have it with me all the time, eating and sleeping, the way the

Arabs do in the book Dad's got on the kitchen shelf." He stroked Cigarette's nose with the unconscious gesture of an automaton. "I'd get a tent and sleep in it myself, and I'd have the colt beside me, and it would have to learn to live just the way I do; and I'd feed it so well it would grow bigger than any other horse on the ranch; and it would be the fastest; and I'd train it so it would follow me wherever I went, like a dog –" At this he paused, struck through and through with bliss at the thought of arousing such devotion in a horse that it would follow him.

There was no warmth yet in the level rays of the sun, and the dawn wind was cold on the mountain side, so that Ken presently began to shiver in his thin dark blue cotton jersey. He turned to face the wind, tasting something of freshness and wildness that went to his head and made him want to run and shout – and ride and ride – to go on all day – as fast as he could and never stop –

He was hatless, and the wind made a tousled mop of his soft straight brown hair, and whipped colour into his thin cheeks that had not yet lost the whiteness of winter school-days. His face was beautiful with the young look of wild-ness and freedom, and his dark blue dreaming eyes.

He must get on Cigarette again.

The moment this thought passed through his mind, Cigarette knew it and turned her head a little to look at him. Her whole body got ready. Not exactly resistant, but waiting.

First he had an apology to make. In all fairness, he must tell Cigarette that the fault had been his own. He had put his heels into her.

He knew exactly what his father would say if he told him about it.

"Cigarette bucked and tossed me."

"What did you do? Put your heels into her?"

"Yes, sir."

He and Howard had to say Yes, sir, and No, sir, to their

father because he had been an Army officer before he had the ranch, and believed in respect and discipline.

Gathering up the rein, slipping it over Cigarette's head, Ken was humming, "Yes, sir – No, sir – Yes, sir – No, sir –" and this seemed to have a soothing effect on Cigarette.

When his father had mounted Cigarette, to show him how, she stood like a statue; never started or jumped; and then had moved off slowly and comfortably like a well-behaved horse in a park. But when *he* mounted her, like as not she would toss him four or five times running, all because he couldn't help trying to grab on with his heels the moment he straddled her. That she wouldn't stand; and that he couldn't help doing.

He turned her so that, on her left side, he was up the hill from her. She was not a tall horse, but even so, the jump from the ground for a boy was a long one, and sometimes his arms didn't pull strongly enough. Last summer he hadn't been able to do it at all, but when he had no saddle must always mount by a fence or from a rock. So far, this summer, he had missed it only a few times.

He took hold of her withers and back, jumped and pulled, landed well up against her, held stiffly there by his arms, then carefully swung his blue-trousered leg over; and slowly, just like his father, settled to her back, legs hanging straight down.

Cigarette was calm. He tightened his rein, squeezed the calves of his legs a little, and she moved off.

One of the exciting things about coming up from school in Laramie to the summer vacation at the ranch, was the weather. Always something doing. Winds and rainbows and calm sunny days, then an electric storm; or frosts or even blizzards. People said it was because of the eight thousand foot altitude.

Now, all the clouds in the sky had caught the sunrise colours, and there was a mingling of pink and red and gold and a keen blue, like electricity, and a wind that was boisterous, like someone scuffling with you, and it played and rippled over the greengrass and made it look like watered silk –

"Greengrass – greengrass –" he chanted, cantering along, thinking how different the greengrass of the range was from the green grass in the little square lawns before the houses down in Laramie, because, on the range, it stretched as far as you could see, and there were jack rabbits hiding in it that sprang up and sailed away over it, riding on the wind with great leaps, as big as small deer. And on the range you called it greengrass, all in one word; and it was important. They read out of the newspaper, "Greengrass in Federal County already," early in the spring. Everyone said, "Have you got greengrass yet? We have."

It was in the spring that it was important, after the last big snow storm in May when all the horses and cattle were so thin and weak from the long winter that it seemed if the greengrass didn't come soon, no one could stand it any longer; and it came first like just a tinge of pale green on the southern and eastern slopes; and the cattle picked and mouthed at it; and soon it was like green velvet; and then, at last, in late June, like this. A sea of rippling grass.

Ken topped the hill and stood staring. From here he looked west over a hundred miles of the greengrass; and south across the great stretch of undulating plateau land that ran down to Twin Peaks, and beyond that across broken crags and interminable rough terrain, mysterious with hidden valleys and gorges and rocky headlands, all the way to the wide farm valleys of Colorado. Beyond them the Neversummer Range stood wrapped in snow winter and summer.

He put his head back and sucked in the smell of the cleanness and the greenness and the snow and the windiness – all so sharp and heavenly.

This was what he had been waiting for. All through the last unbearable months of school, the endless classes, the examinations –

At this an uncomfortable feeling gripped him. His and Howard's reports had arrived in yesterday's mail with a letter from the Principal of the school addressed to their father, Captain McLaughlin. And McLaughlin had slung them on the desk with some papers and bills to open later. By the time Ken got back to breakfast surely his father would have opened them. There was that examination – Ken knew he hadn't done very well –

He wondered what time it was now. He looked down at the ranch.

From his high point of vantage the ground fell away to the north in broken undulations and steppes. Just before it reached the low level of the stream and the meadows a mile away, there was a little gorge in the low hills, bounded by a cliff on the eastern side, and, on the west, a steep hill, both of them covered with thick black pine. In the gorge were cottonwood and young aspen. A stream bed with a thread of water and a road wound through, leading from the stables and horse corrals on the near side, out into a V-shaped clearing beyond the gorge. This, grass covered and studded with young cottonwood trees, his mother called The Green.

Right in the gorge, stretching silver arms up above the trees, and set to catch every stray current of air that sucked through the gully even on windless days, stood the windmill.

On beyond that, in a convenient elbow of the hill to the left, was the bunk house, almost invisible and wonderfully sheltered from winter storms. Farther on down the left side of the V, the long rambling stone ranch house followed the downward slope of the ground by dropping a step from kitchen to dining-room, from dining-room to living-room, and from living-room to study.

Its length was marked by the criss-crosses of the peaked red roofs, by the long, grass-covered terrace along its eastern face, and the low stone wall which upheld it.

There was no sign of life about the place. Too early yet,

thought Ken. Wait — there's smoke coming out of both chimneys. Gus has made the kitchen fire for mother and now he's getting breakfast in the bunk house.

He fastened his eyes on the cow barn. It was the lower boundary of the Green, a vast structure, sinking into the earth to a depth of four feet or more, the gently sloping peaked roof hooding it so closely it left only a ten or fifteen foot strip of whitewashed wall to be seen.

Yellow Guernsey cows were standing about the gate of the corral in the Calf Pasture, to the east. They were waiting for Tim to come and let them in. After they were milked he would let them out of the gate to the north, where they could wander across the meadow to the stream and stand during the heat of the day under the tall cottonwood trees which had their roots down deep under the stream bed.

Far beyond, across the meadows and the hills that sloped up from them, a long freight train was chugging on the railroad tracks. Two toy locomotives, and a toy train. It seemed hardly to move. It was climbing up from the east, going west, soon would cross the top of the Rocky Mountain Divide, and then it would drop its extra locomotive and start down towards the Pacific, and gather speed — and tear along —

An echoing whistle pierced the silence. The train was approaching the Tie Siding crossing.

The cows were moving into the corral — that little black post was Tim, fastening the gate back.

It wouldn't be long before breakfast. Everybody was awake. Going downstairs, his mother would call, "Time to get up boys!" His father was sitting up in bed with his hair rumpled, pyjamas rumpled, hand reaching out for a cigarette.

Gosh — if his father had read the reports! And that wasn't all, there was the saddle blanket too, the lost saddle blanket.

He turned from looking at the ranch house and let his eyes sweep the hillside. Saddle blanket, saddle blanket —

11

every time he asked his father for a colt, McLaughlin said, I'll give you one when you deserve one – not before. It might be caught on a shrub, on a rock – or lying in a gully. Lucky I woke up early. Howard will be sore that I didn't wake him. He always wants to go along. He can never wake up, but I can –

A jack rabbit sprang up almost underfoot. Cigarette jumped, but Ken sat tight, and as the rabbit sailed away, he gave a yell and chased after.

Cigarette loved a good run.

Leaning back as Rob McLaughlin had taught his boys to do, feet forward and out, reins free, Ken rode like a steeple chaser.

Rabbit, pony and boy disappeared over the crest of the Saddle Back.

Chapter Two

Nell McLaughlin pulled the drop-leaf cherry table out from the corner, opened the leaves so that it would comfortably accommodate four people and flung a red-checked cloth over it.

The roomy kitchen was full of bright sunshine from the windows which opened on the front terrace. It made squares of gold on the painted apple-green floor; and in front of sink and stove and baking table there were hooked oval rugs with gay flower patterns. A little brown cat sat by the stove washing her face.

Neither motherhood nor the hard living at the ranch had deprived Nell of her figure or her maidenliness. At thirty-seven she looked not much older than when she had won a silver cup, at Bryn Mawr, for being the best all-round athlete of her class.

Of medium height, with a long slender waist, her curves were held where they belonged by trained muscles, and, as she walked, there was a lightness about her which came

12

partly from natural vigour and partly from the way her narrow head lifted from the shoulders to face whatever was to be faced, a danger, a storm, a loved one, a hope or a fear.

Her skin was tanned to a light fawn colour, not dry and weather beaten, but smooth and with a lustre that came of persistent care; and the thin lips of her rather wide mouth, with clearcut, sensitive curves, were only faintly pink. Her satiny hair, of the same soft fawn colour, fell in a bang over her forehead; the rest was just long enough to be brushed back in shining smoothness and fastened in a little bun in her neck. Riding, she often pulled out the few pins that held it and let it go wild in the wind; and then, with her pale forehead and her dark blue eyes with their wide free look, hers was the face from which Ken's had been copied.

Ken was late to breakfast.

Coming in, he looked first at his father to see if he had opened the reports.

Then he said, "Good morning, Mother, good morning, Dad," pulled out the one empty chair – a green-painted ladder-back chair with seat woven of rawhide thongs – and sat down. His heart was beating hard because his father's face had its glaring look and Howard was smug. Howard always got good marks.

The two boys looked at each other across the table.

Howard was considered the handsome one of the two. His hair was black, like his father's, with a meticulous centre part; and the straight lines of mouth and brows and the bold and somewhat arrogant carriage of his head, made him seem formed and already possessed of a definite character, whereas Ken was unformed, his face sometimes falling into lines of poetic wistfulness and beauty, sometimes like something accidentally assembled – of doubtful promise.

Ken was afraid to look at his father. His blazing blue eyes were hard to meet. They glared at you out of the long, dark face with its jutting chin. Often Ken felt his own eyes

13

reeling back from an encounter, and he would turn away or look down.

McLaughlin picked up a card and a letter which was lying open beside his place. "I suppose it will be no surprise to you to hear that you have not been promoted," he said. "You might like to see your marks."

He tossed the card over to Ken.

Nell McLaughlin handed Ken a blue bowl full of oatmeal covered with cream and brown sugar and said, "Let him eat his breakfast first," but Ken took the card and tried to focus his eyes upon it. He hated so to look, it was hard to see anything at all.

While he studied it there was a silence, Howard eating his bacon and smiling. Nell's face was troubled. She looked down, buttering her toast.

Ken read his marks through and finally came to the English examination.

He looked up and met his father's eye.

McLaughlin leaned forward. "Just as a matter of curiosity," he said, "how do you go about it to get no marks in an examination? Forty in history? Seventeen in arithmetic! But a *zero*! Just as one man to another, what goes on in your head?"

"Yes, tell us how you do it, Ken," chirped Howard.

Nell shot a swift look at her oldest son. "You eat your breakfast Howard," she snapped.

Ken had no answer. His face burned, and he bent over his plate and began on his oatmeal.

McLaughlin pushed away his plate and took out his pipe. There was silence while he filled and lit it, then he picked up the letter and read it aloud.

My dear Captain McLaughlin:

It is with regret that I must tell you that Kenneth's examination marks, averaged with his daily work, do not bring his grades up to passing mark. This is particularly disappointing as his failure is due to carelessness and inattention rather than lack of ability. If he had done even a fair amount of work consistently throughout the school year he would have been promoted into the sixth grade. As it is, he will have to repeat the fifth.

With kind regards to Mrs. McLaughlin and yourself,

Very sincerely,
Leonard Gibson.

McLaughlin put down the letter and looked across the table at Ken, then at his pipe which had gone out.

"Fortunately," he said, reaching for a match, "there are almost two and a half months before school begins again. You'll do an hour a day on your lessons all through the summer to make up this work."

Nell McLaughlin saw Ken wince as if something had actually hurt him, and his eyes went to the wide-open window with a despairing look.

"Well," said McLaughlin, his voice like the crack of a whip. "Speak up. What have you got to say for yourself?"

"I dunno," answered Ken.

"What were you doing in that English exam? What were the questions you missed?"

"We were supposed to write a composition."

"What did you write?"

"I didn't get started."

"Didn't write a word?"

Ken shook his head.

"Couldn't you think of anything?"

"Yes, I had it all planned. I was going to write the story about how you lost your polo mare. How the Albino stole her from Banner —" Ken's eyes went to his father's. "We could write anything we wanted, it had to be at least two pages —"

"Well, what happened to you?"

"I — I — got to thinking about it. Thinking about Gypsy and the Albino — and what it was like, when he took her away — where he took her to — and all the wild horses in his

15

band – and where they were all that time. All of that. I thought there was time, I thought the hour had just begun, and then the bell rang –"

"And you never even started?"

Howard said, "He was looking out the window all the time. I saw him."

Tears were crowding at the back of Ken's eyes. He wished his father would stop looking at him.

There was a knock at the back door and McLaughlin shouted, "Come in."

Gus, the Swedish foreman, came in, carrying his big felt hat in his hand. His thickset body bent in a sort of bow aimed respectfully at Nell, and he looked first of all at her as he said, "Gude mornin', Missus," and then, "Mornin', Boss."

He did not come clear into the room, but propped himself by a hand on the door, leaning there in his shy manner, a little smile like a child's turning up the corners of his mouth. His round pink face was framed in a mop of tight grey curls.

"What's today, Boss?"

Ken and Howard stopped eating to listen.

Only Gus, or perhaps their mother, could ask their father his plans and get an answer. When they asked him, he just said, "Wait and see." Or perhaps would not answer at all. And as every day of the summer was packed with events as thrilling as a circus, they lived much of the time in such suspense that they were ready to burst, dogging their father's steps, trying to be everywhere at once so as to be sure not to miss anything.

Weather always entered into the plans. So before McLaughlin answered, he glanced out the window, noting the clear deep blue of the sky, and that the big white cumulous clouds were sailing across at a rapid pace.

"There's a wind high up in the pines," said Nell. "Heard it the first thing this morning – like surf – a roaring."

16

"And the windmill's goin' lickety split," said Howard.

"Clear for today and mebbe tomorrow," said Gus, "but a big cloud bank in de soudwest. Storm cookin' up."

McLaughlin sat in thought and puffed at his pipe, not at all embarrassed by the fact that four pairs of eyes were watching him and four people waiting for his words.

Finally he said as if to himself, not looking at Gus, "A good day to move the horses."

"*Ja*, Boss. It's time de horses were off de meadows. De grass is growin' an' we should have water on 'em soon."

Howard couldn't keep still. "Could I help you move 'em this year, Dad?"

Ken didn't ask because he had no hope.

McLaughlin turned to look at Howard, but he wasn't thinking of him and did not answer. He smoked and Gus waited. At last he said, "Yes. We've got a month before Frontier Days. I've got to get four of the older horses in shape to rent for the Rodeo. That means fool proof. And those three-year-olds will have to be broken. I can't let them go any longer."

"You're not going to break them yourself, Rob?" said Nell in a loud alarmed voice.

Her husband didn't answer.

"You promised last year!" exclaimed Nell.

"It's my own fault for letting them go so long."

"It's not your fault or anyone's. You haven't time. You haven't help enough to take care of twenty horses, let alone a hundred."

"Well, I can't let them go any longer."

"You shan't do it!" The dark blue of Nell's eyes turned almost black with the widening of the pupils.

"Why, Nell –"

"I can't stand it." Her smooth brown face flushed. "You fighting the horse, and the horse fighting you. Yells and falls and dust and sweat – it makes me sick to see you."

Gus suggested. "Dere's sure to be some good bronco-

17

busters in town 'bout dis time, waitin' for de Rodeo."

McLaughlin frowned. "No bronco-buster is going to break my horses."

"But Rob —"

His voice rose. "It ruins a horse!" He was shouting. This was one of his pet tirades. "He loses something and never gets it back. Something goes out of him. He's not a whole horse any more. I hate the method, waiting until a horse is full grown, all his habits formed, and then a battle to the death, and the horse marked with fear and distrust, his disposition damaged — he'll never have confidence in a man again. And if I lose the confidence of my horses —"

"But they're only three-year-olds," persisted Nell. Howard and Ken looked at her in astonishment. How could she be so fearless in the face of their father's anger and shouting!

There was a soft look about her fawn-coloured hair and smooth, unlined face, but nothing soft about the determined look with which she faced her husband.

"Besides," she said, "they *have* been handled a little, remember; it's not as if they were broncs that had just been pulled in off the range."

McLaughlin sat for a moment or two without reply, then he turned to Gus. "All right, Gus —"

"Can I help you to move 'em, Dad?" said Howard again.

"No," roared McLaughlin. "It's tough enough for one man to move a hundred horses, half of them broncs, or loco, all of them fresh as hell after a winter out, without a kid along to be popping his head up somewhere at just the moment to stampede the bunch!"

"Couldn't I even open the gates for you going down?" said Howard, crestfallen at the thought of missing the long day's riding, the close inspection of all the new spring colts, the exciting trip up on to the summer range on number Twenty with Banner, the big stud, and his band of brood mares.

18

His father ignored the question and turned back to Gus. "You and Tim had better spend the day on the irrigation ditches then. They'll have to be in shape before we turn the water on the meadows."

"*Ja*, Boss."

"And catch up Shorty and saddle him for me. I'll be up at the stables in a half hour or less."

"*Ja*, Boss."

Gus went out.

McLaughlin put down his pipe and pulled his coffee cup towards him. There was a moment's silence, then Howard asked Ken, "What horse did you ride this morning, Ken?"

"Cigarette."

McLaughlin looked up. "You've been riding Cigarette?"

"Yes, sir."

"Did you manage to catch her and tie her up without her breaking anything?"

"No, sir."

"What did she break, a bridle?"

"No – that is – not today. She broke a bridle yesterday."

"What did she break today?"

"The metal catch on the halter rope."

"Haven't I told you you can't tie that mare with one of those? That you have to put a lariat on her?"

"Yes, sir."

"Well, why didn't you?"

"I thought – I thought –" Ken's voice failed him. There weren't any words. He gulped his milk.

"You thought! Trouble is, you don't think."

McLaughlin's voice was gentler.

Howard spoke again. "Did you find the saddle blanket, Ken?"

"What saddle blanket?" asked McLaughlin, on the alert again.

"I lost a saddle blanket out on the range yesterday afternoon when we were riding," said Ken.

19

"Oh, you did?" His father was sarcastic again. "Rode with a saddle, I suppose, and didn't cinch it properly?"

"Yes, sir," said Ken doggedly, "but I found it this morning." There was a quiver in his voice.

"Anything the matter with it?" snapped McLaughlin.

Ken was desperate. "Well, it got a tear; got caught on the barbed wire –"

McLaughlin roared. "What am I going to do with you? You're the stupidest kid for losing and busting and forgetting –"

Ken stared at his plate and felt the heat rising to his face and a lump choking his throat. "Dad – if I only had a colt –"

"What's that got to do with it?"

"Howard's got a colt. He was only nine when you gave him Highboy; and he trained him. I'm ten and even if you did give me a colt now, I couldn't catch up with Howard because I couldn't ride it till it was a three-year-old, and then I'd be thirteen."

Nell laughed. "Nothing wrong with that arithmetic."

But McLaughlin answered. "Howard never gets less than seventy-five average at school. And he pays attention to what I tell him and doesn't lose equipment or break it or get it spoiled somehow."

Ken had no answer to any of this, and kept his eyes down.

"Did Cigarette toss you?" asked Howard cheerfully.

"Yes," answered Ken.

"Did you clap your heels into her?" demanded his father.

"Yes, sir," said Ken automatically.

"Did you rub her down?"

Nothing for it, it was all going to come out. He turned to his father drearily. "I – no, sir, she got away from me."

"Got away from you? Where?"

"Just at the County Road gate, as I was closing it, coming into the Stable Pasture."

"How did it happen?"

"Well, I had the rein in my hand, and I was standing there –"

"What for?"

"Nothing. Just looking around – looking back at the range – and after a while, she wanted to graze and she just gave a little jerk, and she was loose, and then she knew it, and I couldn't catch her. She ran away." Ken felt he might as well tell it all and be done with it. "And she got her foot in the rein and broke it."

"Thought you said you didn't break a bridle today."

Ken hedged, "Well, this wasn't exactly the bridle, it was the rein."

His father unexpectedly made no comment, but looked thoughtfully at Ken. "What were you thinking of when you were standing there by the gate – just standing?"

"My colt."

"*Your* colt! You haven't got a colt."

"The colt I've got in my mind," explained Ken.

"Oh, so you've got one in your mind?"

"Yes, sir."

"Well, you'd better keep it there where it won't run away."

Howard laughed loudly, and McLaughlin knocked the ashes out of his pipe, stuck it in the pocket of his leather vest, and got to his feet.

Ken said desperately, "Won't you give me a colt, Dad?"

McLaughlin paused a moment and looked down at his small son. "You're going to have to buck up, Ken. I don't know what to do with you. You never have your wits about you. "Always wool-gathering. You lose a saddle blanket the first time you go riding –"

"But I found it again –"

"Yes, found the blanket and lost your horse. Trouble is, you don't try."

"I do try."

"I'd like to see some proof of it. Come, Howard. You

can ride with me as far as the meadows and open the gates."

Ken pushed his chair back too. "Can't I help?"

"Certainly not. You have your study to do. Every morning right after breakfast. Remember that."

McLaughlin's scarred boots and heavy spurs clattered across the kitchen floor. Howard strode after, nobly refraining from casting a patronizing glance at Ken.

Nell got her apron and tied it over her short blue-and-white-checked dress. Her bare legs had a smooth coat of sunburn and her small bony feet were neatly shod in brown Mexican huaraches.

Ken stood in a daze, looking at the door that had closed behind his father and Howard.

He felt his mother's hand on his head. She moved it gently, straightening his part. "Kennie," she said, "you can ride any horse on the ranch. Why are you so set on having a colt?"

"Oh, Mother, it isn't just the riding. I want a colt to be friends with me. I want him to be mine – *all my own*, Mother –"

As she looked down into the upturned face, her heart misgave her at the passion and intensity of his longing, but she understood. Yes, she, too, was like that – *all my own* – and she turned away and began to clear the table.

Nell's cat was mewing beside her, begging.

"No, Pauly, this is for the dogs." Nell had some scraps and corn meal mush on a big plate. She handed it to Ken.

"Take it out and feed the dogs, Ken."

Chaps, the fat, curly black cocker, with long hairy chaps on his front legs, was out there, drooling with eagerness. The yellow collie with the white ruff around his neck and the sad brown eyes stood to one side, polite and patient, waving his brush of a tail as he looked at Ken.

Ken put down the plate and went slowly back into the kitchen.

His mother was bustling about. She put a plate of food

near the stove for Pauly, whipped the cover off the table and shook it, let down the drop leaves, and pushed the table over into the corner of the room by the window.

She picked up the little bright oval rugs. "Here, Ken, you might take these out and shake them for me –"

She went to the sink and ran hot water into the dishpan.

Standing there she could look out the door and watch him shaking the rugs slowly – making a game of it – trying to scare the dogs; and it took her back suddenly to when she was a little girl and her mother had made her shake the rugs out of doors after breakfast. That was at the Cape Cod cottage when it had begun to be too hot to stay in Boston –

The water filled the dishpan –

She used to shake them very slowly, one by one, looking around, sniffing the salt tang in the air, listening to the soft boom of the breakers on the beach until her mother's voice inside would call to her to hurry with those rugs –

The hot water was running over and burning her hands –

"Hurry with those rugs, Ken."

He brought them in. "If I could have a colt," he said, like an automaton.

"You go up and do your study now, Ken, and get it over with."

"Where will I put the rugs?"

"Lay them on that chair. I have to sweep the floor yet."

Ken obeyed and walked reluctantly to the door of the dining-room. "Where'll I study?"

"Where are your school books?"

"On the shelf in my room." He went out of the door and she could hear his steps dragging up the stairs.

She sighed. Now, all summer, it'll be the colt, she thought. I wish Howard wouldn't tease him so much. No use speaking to Rob about it, he upholds him – says Ken has to take it – I'd make Howard shut up – wish Rob would give him a colt –

She dried the dishes rapidly and put them away.

There was no kindling, and she ran out to the woodpile behind the house, and seized the hatchet, swinging it as lustily as if it had been a racket on the tennis court.

It's a good thing Gus isn't around, she thought. The other day Gus had caught her cutting wood and had gently taken the axe from her hand. "T'ree men on de place and you cut your own wood, Missus? No – no, not while old Gus is here –"

It had amused Nell at first to be addressed as the *Missus*, but it had not taken her long to learn that, here in the West, it meant "the woman", with all that the word signified of gentleness and motherliness. Here, in her world of men, husband and sons, hired men, haying crew, horse buyers, to be the *Missus* meant to be that before which they could remove their hats, and bend their heads. In the cities a woman could turn into a driving machine, or harden herself to meet difficulties, but the Missus on a farm or ranch, though she might be milker of cows or trainer of horses, must be more and not less woman for all that, or she would rob the men around her of something which was as sweet to them as the sugar in their coffee.

She carried in her kindling, filled the basket beside the stove, and took up the broom. Through the window she caught sight of a great tumbleweed bounding across the Green, and stood still, watching, her lips parted and her eyes alight. She heard the jack pines roaring – like surf, she thought, yes, like the sea. She could see them bending and swinging in the wind. It was a day when she wanted to be outdoors, riding on the range, where the wind would whip her hair and drive her the way it drove the tumbleweed across the Green.

But first, sweeping, bed-making, cleaning, the noon dinner – She began to sweep, singing,

> Oh, the ship she sailed,
> Across the sea,
> Good-bye, my lover, good-bye –

Chapter Three

When Ken left the kitchen the alarm clock on the wall shelf beside the spice closet pointed to twenty minutes to nine. He wondered if he should time himself right from then or from the moment he went into his room, or from when he set his books on the table. This was a very important point, but as he could not decide, he went upstairs as slowly as he could, just in case it was all part of the hour.

He paused on the landing in front of the picture of the duck. If he stood there looking at the duck picture he could get into another world. He knew how to do it. To get into another world you had to make yourself the same size, in your mind.

When he put his face down to the little pools in the stream and stayed there a long time, pretending that he was one of the little crabs that scuttled from rock to rock, or a baby trout smaller than a minnow, pretty soon he was

25

right in that world under the water and could almost know why they moved about and went up so seriously to meet each other, talked a moment, then hurried away.

It was one of the most exciting things, to get into another world than your own regular world, especially at a time when the regular world or the things you had to do in it bored you. Like now.

But he felt misgivings, standing there. His mother would hear, from the kitchen, that he hadn't gone all the way upstairs. He went on up, down the hall, into his room, and noisily closed the door. Possibly she would time him too.

He looked at the alarm clock that stood on his dresser – almost ten minutes to nine – funny –

He stood a few moments looking around. He and Howard each had a small room to himself.

Ken loved his room. The walls were white-washed, and there was a big window opening out front over the terrace and the Green. He could see everything from it. Sunshine poured in.

Best of all, Ken loved his little walnut bed, because that was really home. Everything was home in a way except school. The United States of America was home and he could feel it when they sang *The Star-Spangled Banner*. And the ranch was home. The house was home. But most particularly the bed was home. It was like friendly arms close around him every night when he got into it.

It wasn't very tidy. He and Howard had to make their own beds, and he had made his in a hurry, before he went out riding. Now would be a good time to straighten it up. That was a good dutiful deed – about as good as studying – it probably could be counted in the hour. The quilt, which was light green with sprigs of pink and blue flowers on it, was crooked and humped over the bedclothes underneath. He threw it back, then paused, his eyes on the wall at the head of the bed.

There were these pictures – one on each side – about eight inches square, with a flat wooden frame an inch wide.

And inside the frame —

He dropped the quilt, moved up to one picture and stood minutely examining it. What people! Peasant people, his mother had told him, probably Swiss.

They were dressed very oddly. The man had a white shirt, embroidered suspenders, a tilted hat with a feather in it, short pants to his knees, and a flute in his hand!

The woman had a white waist, laced black bodice, full skirt, a handkerchief over her head, and she was sitting on a ledge which jutted into a stream with her bare legs and feet in the water. She was leaning over, reaching her arms to hold a little naked boy who stood in the stream and leaned against her, frightened, it seemed, and lifting one foot out of the water because a big duck with a flock of baby ducks was paddling about, cruising close to his legs. Under the boy's mop of hair, exactly the same yellow as the ducklings, his face looked around, quite frightened. His eyes were very blue and his cheeks fat and red. His mother smiled indulgently.

His father, behind them, seemed protecting them, and sat watching and ready to play the flute.

Ken had never been in such a world as that.

He climbed across the bed and looked at the other picture which was another peasant picture, but inside a house.

Down at the end of his room was the strangest picture of all.

Ken went to look at it. There was a verse written in the corner which he knew by heart.

> Intreat me not to leave thee,
> Nor to return from following after thee.
> For whither thou goest I will go,
> And where thou lodgest I will lodge.

It was a picture of a desert land. And a man stood as if waiting to go, looking at the maiden for whom he was wait-ing. But she had run back to throw her arms around a

27

woman, and there they stood, arms about each other. And the verse in the corner was what she was saying. They were dressed in long, draped, brightly coloured shawls.

"Intreat me not to leave thee," he murmured, liking something about the way the words made his voice rise and fall. Besides, there was something in this picture that the other pictures did not have, something completely grown-up and mysterious and a little exciting.

"Intreat me –" He jumped and ran back to the bed when he heard quick steps across the kitchen floor below. Outside the kitchen door his mother's voice called, "Here, Kim – Here, Chaps –"

This time he really finished the bed and smoothed the quilt. It looked very nice. He stood regarding it, thinking that now he must take down his books.

His desk was in the corner near the window. It was just a table with a few drawers, and over it hung a wall bracket with three shelves. The study books were not the only books on it. There were some fairy books. There was "Castle Blair" – and what a world that let you into – a whole gang of children that lived in a castle in Scotland. Ken knew it as well as they did. And there was "At the Back of the North Wind". And there was –

He was just scanning the titles. He sighed deeply. He didn't feel very well and wondered if perhaps he was going to be sick.

Resolutely he picked out his arithmetic book, sat down, opened it and began to think.

Shorty – ugly brown Shorty with mops of hair on his hoofs and his forehead, and legs so short his father had said he was built like a dachshund –

But he always rides Shorty when there's something hard to do, thought Ken. Howard's got Highboy. Wonder if they're saddled yet. Bet I could do a round-up all alone if I could have Shorty. He does it just about all himself, he always knows better than anybody else where the horses are when you're hunting for them – wonder how he does that, smells them I guess – and he knows which way they're headed, and he takes a short cut and gets there ahead of them. Wonder why he likes to do that? He's a horse too, and he ought to be on their side and not help catch them – guess it's like playing tag. Dad says Shorty's the smartest horse on the ranch, but I don't like him. He's kinda mean. I like Banner better –

Ken's eyes took on a vacant look as in imagination he pictured the big golden chestnut stallion who sired the early crop of twenty colts. All the youngsters, three-year-olds, twos, yearlings, and now the little foals, were his.

Banner was like a king. He had never been ridden, but he and Rob McLaughlin were friends and understood each other. Nell said that until she had come to the West she had never known how nearly human a stallion could be.

Ken had seen his father and Banner standing close, facing each other, Banner's ears taut, his nose stretched out with nostrils distended as they tried to breathe in the very essence of the man they reached for, and his legs stiff and trembling a little. He didn't like to get too close to people.

His father's legs were stiff too and braced apart, the way he often stood, and his arms were folded, and his round head with the tight curled black hair tilted back and he talked in a low, even voice that no one but Banner could hear, as if they were making plans.

Banner and his father together ran the ranch.

Suddenly Ken heard the sound of horses coming near the house and started up so quickly that the leg of his chair tangled with the leg of the table and he went sprawling on the floor, then scrambled up and over to the window. There they were. Chaps was along too. Chaps and Shorty were crazy about each other. Shorty always liked to have Chaps along. Chaps had so much sense. Kim wasn't there. Locked up, probably. He made trouble. He looked like a coyote and some of the colts were afraid of him.

29

Chaps was jumping up and down right under Shorty's nose, practically under his feet. When he did that, it always looked as if he was nipping his nose. Shorty didn't mind. Perhaps that was their way of kissing. But Banner minded – Chaps had to keep away from the stallion.

Ken leaned out the window as far as he could to see the last of them as they went down the Green, just jog-trotting, and disappeared around the end of the house –

"Ken!" Nell's voice came floating up from the open window below. "What are you doing?"

He scurried back to the table and made it true before he answered, "I'm doing my arithmetic."

"What was that crash?"

"My chair fell over."

"What made it fall over?"

"It just fell over – "

Nothing more from Nell, and Ken summoned all his energy and frowned at his open book. He must make a plan. He would do cancellation over. He liked cancellation. It was fun crossing out the figures above and below the line and turning everything into nothing.

He hunted for his pad, opened all the drawers, and found it.

Then he heard Nell coming up the stairs, and she opened his door.

She had some fresh bureau scarves over her arm, and came in briskly and went to his chiffonier to change the scarf.

"I was thinking, Ken, it would be a good idea if you spent your study hour on that composition."

"The composition?"

"Yes, the one you didn't write. If you wrote it nicely we could send it to Mr. Gibson and tell him how it was you came not to write anything – that you were think-ing about it – and he might let you have some credit for it."

"The one about the Albino," said Ken, and his eyes

went thoughtfully to the window. "How would I begin it?"

"Have you got paper there?"

"Yes."

"Well, just pretend you're telling someone about it — someone who doesn't know. Me, for instance. Perhaps I've forgotten. Who was the Albino, anyway?"

Ken grinned, and said, "A big white stallion — just a bronc — who came over the border from Montana when they had a drouth there. Dad called him a big ugly devil but a lotta horse — "

"That's fine," encouraged Nell. "And what did he do?"

"Stole everybody's mares, and when they had a spring round-up six years later they caught him and the whole bunch of mares and everyone around here found some mares they had lost, and the Albino had taken Gypsy — "

"Who was Gypsy?"

"Dad's polo mare that he had in the Army and he had put her in the brood mare bunch and he was counting on getting a lot of good colts from her — "

"Yes?"

"But the Albino stole her, or she ran away to him. And when they caught them both in the round-up, Gypsy was there too, with four colts, and Dad brought 'em all back to the ranch. And the colts were beauties, and fast and strong, but wild as anything. And Dad sold the two horse colts and put the fillies in the brood mare bunch, but he never could break them. He said the Albino was bad blood. Loco. Rocket's one of them. She was the best of the four."

"And what about Gypsy. Is she still alive?"

"She's twenty-three years old, and she hasn't got many teeth and she's kinda poor now 'cause she can't chew so well, but she has a colt 'most every year, and good ones too."

"Now you see, Ken, that would make a very good composition. And you could call it 'The Story of Gypsy.' "

She came to the back of his chair and stood there.

"You begin it now, dear."

"The hour is nearly up."

"You can finish it tomorrow."

Ken sighed deeply, and wrote, "The Story of Gypsy," carefully at the top of the paper.

Nell went out of the room and he heard her open the door of the upstairs closet and take the carpet sweeper out of it, and go into her own room and begin to sweep the floor.

He lifted his head and listened for sounds that came from farther away. How far had they got down the road? How would Banner behave with Shorty around? Stallions didn't like geldings – didn't like anything but mares – Banner –

The hovering pencil drew a long horse face – two sharp ears on the alert – and began on a wind-tossed mane.

Ken tore down the road. He'd take the short cut. They'd been gone almost an hour and they were on horseback. He'd meet them about halfway coming back maybe, and see the whole bunch moving. He'd find a good place and hide so his father wouldn't see him.

He trotted along in the irrigation ditch. It was dry because the water hadn't been turned in yet. This way he would avoid the road and the gates. Howard might be stationed at any one of the gates.

He kept a sharp look-out. Not a horse in sight anywhere. Now if I had my horse, I'd be riding. We could canter along in the ditch here.

A tangle of briars and chokecherry bushes grown over the ditch blocked his way and he fought his way through. When the ditch was crossed by the barbed wire fences he got down on his hands and knees and crawled under.

He was winded. He always lost his breath easily when he first came up to the ranch after the winter in Laramie.

He slowed down and plodded along. It seemed a long way.

He left the ditch and climbed up a hill. From here he could see Gus and Tim working in the ditch in the Crooked Meadow and could hear their voices. Tim was swinging a pick; the sound of the blow reached him after he saw the pick land.

And a mile or more away he could see Castle Rock, the great beetling rock, jutting up seventy feet high, with peaks and parapets and turrets shaped like a castle. It overhung the aspen grove at the far end of the meadow.

That was where they were, down there near the rock. His father was rounding up the mares with their foals, getting them out of the woods, bringing them back through the meadow slowly. He never ran them. He'd keep them walking slowly all day, let them stop to graze. He said scornful things about riders who galloped and yelled and drove horses on the run.

Ken ran down the hill and headed for the big rock. He ran as far as he could and then stopped to get his wind again and make a calculation.

From where he was now, on the grazing land which sloped down to the barbed wire fence around the meadow, he could see the wide gate open and fastened back. That was so the mares could come through up to where he was. There was a sort of road here, and the mares would follow it naturally and stay right on it. It curved north and then east across the grazing land, and then merged with the road that led from the Lincoln Highway to the ranch. Probably his father would take them that way, through the Green and the Gorge up to the stables and give them all a feed of oats there before he took them on through the Stable Pasture and out on to the Saddle Back.

If he could hide somewhere near here, where he could keep his eye on the gate, he'd see them pass quite close.

He looked about for shelter. Here and there was a jagged outcropping of the pink granite which underlay the soil, here and there a small clump of wild currant bushes.

He chose the bushes, dropped down behind one and sat panting. He could get his wind now.

What a lot of time they were taking. He put his head around the bush and looked and listened, but there was not a sound, nor could he see any of the mares down in the meadow. They must all be in the aspen grove at the end, hidden by the trees and big rocks.

He drew back behind the bush and lay down and suddenly felt very tired and very happy. The report and the saddle blanket and the study – all the unpleasant things – were behind him; and the grass he was lying on smelled sweet; and he was going to see his father and Banner bring the brood mares and foals up from the meadow. The sky was close, and the blue curved over him – up here at the ranch you could always see the curve – it wasn't flat. The clouds were solid looking, with definite strange shapes, and the wind was driving them across the sky – in a moment he was sound asleep.

He woke with a jerk, coming up from such a deep place that it seemed he must have slept for hours.

He was bewildered and sat up, trying to gather his wits. Then he remembered and scrambled to his feet – would he be too late? – they might have passed while he was asleep – he ran out from behind the bush – head on into the bunch.

The mares were coming up from the meadow, almost noiselessly on the grass, McLaughlin in the rear, and Banner offside in the middle. They were walking as quietly as the cows coming in for milking.

In the lead was a powerful, long-legged mare with a shiny black coat. She carried her nose in the air, her wild, staring eyes ringed with white. Rocket, the loco mare, daughter of the Albino.

As Ken shot out from behind the bush, almost colliding with her, she snorted in terror and went straight up on her hind legs.

For a moment Ken was under the dangling black hoofs

of her forelegs and smelled the heat of her body, then she twisted to one side, made a great leap and shot away, and it seemed to Ken that it was a hundred horses that leaped and scattered after her, instead of just twenty.

The foals were terrified. They wheeled and galloped beside their mothers, holding themselves close as if an invisible cord bound them.

Ken could see nothing but the legs and bodies of horses pounding past him, and the smaller, shadow-like shapes of the foals. Then he heard his father shouting, and the long-drawn cry, "Whoa – whoa – whoa there –" that carried so far and had such power to quiet the horses, but this time it was as if they did not hear him.

Ken ran to a pile of rocks and scrambled to the top so he could see all that happened.

Rocket had gone off at an angle to the line of march and was on a dead run, stretched out like a race horse, with the whole bunch after her. She was heading for the Rock Slide, a place where the grazing land broke down to the lower levels of the next pasture over a long curving hill of sheer rock. To go down it on foot, he and Howard had to sit and slide. No horse, not even the most sure-footed, could negotiate that drop. If she went over she'd go head over heels, she'd roll and bounce to the bottom, and all the others too, if they followed her, the whole band of mares and colts pitching down, somersaulting, rolling, crashing –

"Whoa – there – whoa – whoa –" McLaughlin's voice rang out on a note of desperation. He was galloping as fast as he could to head off Rocket, but she had a long lead and Shorty was slow.

Ken groaned. The Rock Slide – that black fury, Rocket – *running fool* – and for once his father's voice powerless –

Then Ken saw the big stallion, Banner, shoot out of the crush. His bright chestnut coat was like flame in the sunlight. His feet thundered.

"Oh, go it, Banner – go it!" shouted Ken in an agony, dancing up and down on his rock.

Banner's ears were flat back, his head dropped low to the ground and elongated so that it seemed an extension of his neck. He had a look of fury. Nothing made the stud so mad as to have a mare break out of the bunch when he was in charge. If he could catch Rocket he'd half kill her –

The two horses were running at an angle to each other, Banner gaining. They converged near the Rock Slide. Banner's head was suddenly right over Rocket's, his golden mane mingled with her black mane, his mouth open and his big teeth bared.

Suddenly his jaws snapped and Rocket gave a furious squeal and stopped with a jar. Banner whirled and lashed and his heels struck her side with a ringing smack. The other mares telescoped up against them.

Then Banner was everywhere at once, biting, driving, wheeling and kicking the mares back. As they milled around he dropped his head again and charged them, swinging back and forth in long semi-circles, until he had got them turned and moving in the other direction, back up the grazing land towards the road.

Not one single mare lost – not a colt hurt or crushed – Rocket herself, panting and foam flecked, walking meekly back towards the road –

Ken's terror was now for himself. If his father should see him! He might not have. Might have thought it was something else that scared them, a coyote, or perhaps just Rocket's craziness.

He slid down the rock and sat hunched up at the base of it. He was fairly well hidden there, rocks and currant bushes all around him.

His hands were cold and trembling with the awfulness of what he had done and of what the loss of the brood mares, or even a few of them, would have meant to his father.

36

He could hear the pounding of the horses' hoofs going farther away and he began to breathe more easily. Then a shadow fell on him and he looked up and saw his father sitting there on Shorty.

After one look into the blazing eyes under the down-drawn brim of the Stetson hat, Ken dropped his head and sat silent.

"I – I just came to see the horses," he murmured at last.

McLaughlin said nothing.

Ken looked up again and the look on his father's face made him burn all over.

He cried out sharply, "I didn't mean to do it, Dad – I didn't mean to scare them –"

He wanted to go on and explain that he had fallen asleep and then run out to see if they had gone – and Rocket was right there. But there wasn't time. Without a word of answer or blame, McLaughlin wheeled Shorty and went cantering away after the mares.

Ken felt as if he had been put out of the ranch, out of all the concerns that Howard was in on. And out of his father's heart – that was the worst. What he was always hoping for was to be friends with his father, and now this, so soon after getting home – His despair made him feel weak. He put his head down on his drawn-up knees and his hands were clenched tight.

After a while he slid down flat and slept again; a deep exhausted sleep this time that made up the hours he had lost riding so early that morning.

It was long after noon when the faraway cry of a hawk, harsh and sad, drew him up to wakefulness; and he opened his eyes directly into the blue of the sky and saw the hawk wheeling against it.

The wind had gone down. The hawk circled and cried again. Ken yawned deeply and lay there, watching the hawk, his arm lying in the currant bush.

At last he sat up against the rock. His eyes wandered,

taking in everything with an absent, unconscious look.

Not twelve feet away the long neck and head of an ermine came up through a gopher hole at the foot of a rock. The soft fur was dun-coloured, like the earth. Except for the little movement, and unless you had been looking right there, you could never have seen him. It was like a miniature periscope. Neck and head were the same size, as if there were eyes and an infinitesimal pair of ears on the neck itself. As it looked around the whole neck rotated. Presently it was looking right at Ken, seeing him. After a moment's calm inspection it withdrew its head and disappeared.

Ken sat, gathering up the threads that stretched from the events behind him to the events ahead. He would have to meet his father and everyone; they would all know that he had almost stampeded the mares over the Rock Slide.

Of course, now, he couldn't get to be friends with his father.

And he wouldn't get a colt this summer.

The hawk circled lower and cried again, but Ken didn't hear it. It swung down close, spreading six feet of brown feathered wings, curled talons reaching for the rock.

As the shadow fell on him, Ken looked up and gave a great start, and the hawk flapped its wings violently, and slid off sideways.

Ken got to his feet and started home.

If he couldn't have a real colt, at least he could have a make-believe. His eyes changed expression. Maybe one like Rocket – black and shiny with her nose up in the air and her tangled mane and tail streaming, and the very wickedness and wildness of her –

Or Banner – the gloriousness of his rush after Rocket – the way he made all the mares mind him – the long snaky head, the blazing gold of his hide – as bright as the coals in the stove –

Ken's mouth opened a little, smiling.

Chapter Four

Banner had got his name when he was a two months' old colt, on the day that Nell first saw him.

She was riding alone on the Saddle Back one August afternoon, cantering easily, twirling a short strip of soft leather in her right hand. The prevailing southwesterly wind of the Rocky Mountains sang in her ears and moved like a veil between earth and sky; her white silk shirt filled and ballooned; her hair was loose and blowing, and the grass on the hillsides leaned and rippled and sprang erect again with an incessant murmuring sound.

Hay was being cut somewhere, and the strong aromatic scent of it – the late summer scent of hay and mint and pine and snow – had a keen edge of sweetness to it that hurt her lungs. Miles away, a rancher was shouting at his horses, and the sound drifted to her like an echo, made musical and poignant by the distance. Lost in delight, she

39

twirled her quirt, swaying a little to the rhythmic thud of her pony's hoofs; and she had such a sensation of lightness it seemed to her that on this high peak of the Divide, the world was curled in a wave – herself carried on the rolling crest of it like foam.

Suddenly the grey gelding she rode pricked his ears. She was approaching the brood mares. Around the shoulder of a hill she came upon them, already on the alert, facing towards her, heads up nervously. Nell stopped her horse and sat watching. Some of them galloped away – the colts clinging to their mothers' sides – then stopped at a distance and turned to stare again.

A rich dark chestnut colt, fearless and adventuresome, broke out of the bunch and came towards her with a long springing trot. There was a very fury of curiosity and expectation in his lifted head and flaring nostrils. His cream-coloured tail was lifted high, pluming out on both sides of him, and with the full tossing light mane, he seemed to float on the wind, hung with banners.

And so he got his name, and was duly registered and raised to be the stud of Goose Bar Ranch. Banner, out of the Arab mare El Kantara, by Hamilcar.

With the passing years, his dark chestnut coat had grown lighter, and the blond tail and mane darker, so that now in full maturity, the stallion was a bright red-gold all over. The name still suited him. He had lost nothing of his wild grace and ardour, and, trotting, still came on the wind, full sail set, head up, and the high, free springing step.

When the moon rose that night, after the long journey with the mares up to the summer range, the stallion was standing, as he often did, on the sharp rocky peak of one of the hills of the Saddle Back, slanted as if on a stair, with forefeet solid and close together on the summit, his long gleaming body sloping down, his lofty head and reaching ears the very picture of kingly power.

Round about him and beneath him on all sides was a wider world than even his swiftness could ever need or use; the same world of hills and plains, plateaus and head-lands, mesas and mountains that Ken had filled his eyes with that morning.

Within a radius of a few hundred yards below him were his twenty-odd mares and their foals, now weary from the day's long trek up from the meadows. Some of them were grazing, some lying flat on their sides in an ungainliness of abandon which was grotesque in the mares, but in the foals had a charming helplessness. Cushioned on the springing greengrass, earth and horse as close as two hands with palms pressed together, they lay sleeping under the eye of the watchful stallion.

A sudden thunder of hoofs pulsed on the air and drifted away again. Instantly Banner's head turned and his ears pointed. A mile or more away the band of yearlings was on the run. Something had startled them; or with their crazy high spirits they were just tearing around, turning night into day.

Closer by, a frightened little whinny shrilled out, not much more than a squeal of alarm. A foal, grazing too far from his mother, had come to with a start, alone and terrified, his world shattered.

Banner calmly watched the long-legged youngster while he galloped to one mare after the other, sniffed them, and squealed his disappointment.

At last the placid mother lifted her head from her grazing and called him. The little one halted in mid-gallop, wheeled, nickered, and ran to her side, thrusting his head immediately beneath her.

And at last Banner twisted his massive neck and looked in another direction – down at the ranch where lived his god.

Oats.

The smell of the big, hard, muscular hand that held the bucket.

The harsh voice that pierced his vitals.

All this went with the greatest goodness that he had ever known. His world went no further. Together, he and Rob McLaughlin ran the ranch. In the fall the two would separate the spring colts from their dams and Banner would bite and kick and drive the mares away while McLaughlin penned the colts. In the worst of the winter blizzards, Banner would bring the mares home from five or ten miles away, knowing that McLaughlin would have been before him to open gates and doors and fill the manger of the feed shed with hay. Now and then Banner had to do or endure something he could not understand. This too he accepted. When Rob McLaughlin's blazing blue eyes commanded, Banner looked no farther.

Now, smoke was coming from the chimney of the ranch house.

Banner saw it and smelled it. It was a familiar, good smell. His ears quivered, taut and listening. Often voices, shouts, barking of dogs, the piano, the radio, reached him in a medley of sounds, all good. All Rob, and shelter and food and companionship. But tonight, no sound but the chug of the windmill pump.

Banner swung his head back again and stood straight, facing the moon. The golden fire that was in his eye when he was alert died down and his lids half closed.

Nell too was watching the moon rise.

She was standing at the living-room door, looking out across the terrace and the Green.

It was a Dutch door, cut horizontally in half, like a stable door; and Nell's elbows were propped on the top of the lower part. Leaning over a little she rested her smooth sun-burned cheeks in her hands.

She had been riding that afternoon, and was still in her black jodhpurs and white silk shirt.

Dead tired, as she often was at night, she told herself that she had letters to write, and she must set the sponge

42

for tomorrow's baking; but she just stood there, leaning, and looking across the Green.

She was thinking about Ken and what he had done that day and how furious Rob had been.

Nothing had been said about it to Ken.

Howard always took his cue from his father, so he too ignored Ken. They talked about the mares, the colts, and how long the grass was, and which mares had not yet foaled, and the old piece of lariat that was still tied around Rocket's neck, from the time, more than a year before, when Rob had tried to get Rocket in the chute and Rocket had broken three lariats in succession. Nell had had to drive into town to buy new ropes, until, in Cheyenne, they were asking, "What kind of an outlaw is the Captain trying to break?"

The reason McLaughlin had given up trying and had let her go was because she kicked to pieces the little wooden coop which led into the chute, and had so injured her hocks and legs that he was afraid she would be ruined.

"I've always worried about that noose around her neck," Rob said at supper. "It might choke her someday. Get caught in a branch or wire. Never turn an animal out with a rope or even a halter on – not if it's to run wild for a long time."

"What if it did choke her?" asked Howard. "You always say she's no use to you."

"There's a responsibility we have towards animals," said his father. "We use them. We shut them up, keep their natural food and water away from them, that means we have to feed and water them. Take their freedom away, rope them, harness them, that means we have to supply a different sort of safety for them. Once I've put a rope on a horse, or taken away its ability to take care of itself, then I've got to take care of it. Do you see that? That noose around her neck is a danger to her, and I put it there, so I have to get it off."

Ken had not talked at all but ate his supper in silence.

At bedtime, when he came to kiss his mother good night, she put her hand on his head, and he pressed his forehead against her for a moment, then kissed her quickly and went to kiss his father. Then up to bed.

Something's simply got to be done, thought Nell. I wish Rob would give him a colt.

Across the Green, the Hill was a black silhouette against a luminous fan of moonlight that was spreading behind it. The pines were motionless. It was a calm, brooding night. The line of the Hill climbed to the right and became the cliff overhanging the Gorge. To the left it ran down to nothing and joined the Calf Pasture. The young cottonwoods on the Green, about a dozen of them that Rob had planted, were swaying. They were never quite still. The round sphere that the mass of their leaves made floated on the air with a faint whispering sound. They were a lighter green than anything else, like a girl's fairness against the black-bearded Hill.

What tons of water it had taken to make them grow. They had carried water in buckets – dozens, hundreds of buckets of water from the spring – and poured on their roots. And even so, many of them had died and new ones had to be put in. Rob was always having to put in new little cottonwoods. They would never have been their if it hadn't been for his determination. In the fall their leaves turned pale gold and drifted off the trees, and whirled about on the Green in little cyclones and curling eddies. I'm glad I've got the Green, she thought. Like the village Greens home in New England. This is really like the East. No, not the East. The East is cosy. There is never the distance, the fat, empty distances – the wide loneliness. Miles and miles before you come to another house. Just animals. Grass and animals and sky. You can smell the loneliness. No – it's the emptiness you can smell. Of course, you can smell that. It *is* empty. Other places, the land is full of houses and factories and towns and people and people's doings. But this is almost a desert. And it has

44

this sweet, fresh, singing, wildness – you can breathe it in, the very moment you wake in the morning. And it lifts you. You could just float out the window into the blue of the sky, young and new like the country.

It's just the house that's like the East. A New England country house made of pink stone. Not like the western ranch houses. They're like ugly workshops. Untidy. Old wrecks of machines dumped anywheres. Tumble-down buildings leaning together. No time, I suppose, not an ounce of energy or a minute of time left over from the awful, hopeless struggle to make a living. Sun in the wrong place where it scorches and burns and exhausts you. Black shade where you want sun and warmth. No comfort. The buildings lie in a heap, as if they'd been thrown there – and there they stay.

She raised her head and sniffed. The flower border below the terrace wall was crammed with iris and forget-me-nots and larkspur and lilac and petunias. It was the lilac scent that drenched the evening air. Fancy lilac as late as this – in New England it would have been over long ago.

She felt two tiny paws against the leg of her jodhpurs. Pauly gave a little pleading meow. When Nell paid no attention she proceeded to climb up her leg, hooking her claws into the cloth. At about the belt line, Nell, in self defence, caught hold of her and lifted her to sit on her left arm. This was the cat's favourite seat. She looped her right arm around Nell's neck, holding on with a velvet paw which never permitted the tip of a claw to emerge.

Nell straightened up with a sigh, leaned her cheek against Pauly and smoothed the soft fur. Then she got her sewing basket and Ken's torn saddle blanket, and went to sit close beside Rob's desk in his study, where he was working at his accounts.

Chapter Five

The big gasoline lamp on the top of Rob's desk laid a circle of brightness on the gloom of the room and enclosed them both.

Nell sat with one foot under her. Her fine, narrow head was bent over her work and her hair shone like fawn-coloured satin in the lamplight. She had been careful of her hands with their long pointed fingers and almond shaped nails, and they were as smooth as the brown eggs that came from the Rhode Island Red hens. When she talked, she gestured with them, and they had that artless look, the lack of any clutch or grasp, the question in the bent back, reaching finger tips, which always suggests a poetic nature.

Rob often watched them, thinking that they moved like something that was helpless, seaweed floating – Ken had the same hands. They didn't take hold. But now, weaving the blue wool in and out the torn saddle blanket, Nell's hands were quick and deft.

Between stitches she glanced at her husband, his round head, with the tight cap of black hair, had the hardness of a profile on a coin. Presently she said, "Rob – give Kennie a colt."

Rob made no answer. He might not have heard. Sitting at his desk, before him a pile of bills and a scratch pad on which he was jotting figures, he was silent and absorbed.

Bills, thought Nell. I wonder which one, particularly. He's worried these days. Always figuring, always accounts, he hates it too, hates figures as much as Ken hates 'em – never used to do it.

This thought escaped into speech. "You never used to keep so many accounts, Rob."

This got an answer, as his pencil jotted down a total and

scored a heavy line. He leaned back with a short laugh.

"Never knew I'd have to." He stretched wearily, then reached for the pipe lying on the ash tray, and opening his pen knife, he began to scrape it out.

"Are we broke?"

"We're – just two jumps ahead of –" His voice trailed into silence, and Nell's eyes flitted wildly for a moment, as if she would find the pursuing menace lurking in some dark corner of the house.

"But haven't we always been? Is it any worse?" she asked.

He grinned a little. "For a long time I didn't know it," and he took out his tobacco pouch.

"Know what?"

"That each year I was worth less money, instead of more."

"Is it really like that, Rob?"

"It is. A rancher or a farmer can't know whether he is operating at a profit or a loss unless he makes a very careful yearly inventory. I read that in a Government Bulletin once. That's what pulled me up. You can see why it's true. Equipment deteriorates, buildings run down, there are stock losses, indebtedness increase; but it's all so gradual, almost imperceptible, a man doesn't notice it. He drifts along, thinking that things are about as they always were. You see it all around here. Some poor devil trying to renew a loan, or get a new one he badly needs, and finding out he hasn't got anything left that the banks will lend on. He's been on the down grade for a long time – he never knew it. It hits him all of a sudden. He's a bankrupt – and the day before, he thought he was a capitalist. Well – I take the trouble, now, to know where I stand."

"And is it? Are we on the down grade?"

"We are."

"But we're more and more careful all the time. We spend less; don't have as much help – why, we're actually stingy –"

"In the beginning I still had some capital – what was left over when I bought the ranch. I was going to save that – should have. It would have sent the boys to college. But now that's gone. Of course I thought that when I got the horses well started – when they were of an age to sell, I'd make it all back and more, but expenses always keep ahead of me. With so many pure-bred horses, for instance, and more coming all the time, there are such walloping taxes."

This always made Rob angry. It's a cock-eyed law – to put high taxes on registered stock – it ought to be the other way around. They ought to tax out of existence this run-down mongrel stuff that Wyoming is full of. It would be better for the state if they did. I wish I had nothing but registered horses. These colts of Gypsy and the Albino have put a bad strain into my stock."

He sat scowling for a moment, and then said, "The worst thing of all is, I can't sell my horses at a profit. Not even at cost, most of the time."

This struck a chill through Nell. Everything depended on the horses.

"Perhaps the markets will get better –" she said, but her voice reflected the fear in her heart.

Rob struck the back of his hand angrily on the desk. "A thing like this – Doc Hicks' bill – this gets me. He can't help it. I'm not blaming him, but here it is. Three visits at fifteen dollars each, and even then the mare died –"

He leaned back and puffed at his pipe and Nell darned in silence.

"Bad enough to pay veterinary bills when they get well, although you don't know if you'll ever sell the animal for enough to pay you back for all he's cost. But when they die! By God, I'll not do it again. Sick or well they can take their chances. They get well when you do nothing for them, and give them up; they die when you get the vet and nurse them."

Often, when Rob talked like this, a tide of fear rose in

48

Nell's heart. It was almost panic. Oh, Rob, Rob, what'll we do? If you'd only stayed in the Army – if you'd only never bought the ranch – but you would have it – you're like Ken. When you set your heart you can't give up – just because you were so crazy about horses, and such a fine rider at West Point –

Her eyes were hidden from him. Lids down, she watched the thread weaving in and out the blue blanket, and there was no tremor of her hands to show him that she was frightened – had been frightened for years –

"Doc'll have to wait for his money," said Rob. "I'll owe it to him – and some more added to it. I've got nine two-year-olds for him to geld."

"When's he coming?"

"Sometime this week. I told him to come any day. I've got the colts in. Poor devil, I don't see how he lives. Nobody pays him. Nobody can afford to."

"Rob, doesn't *anybody* make money ranching?"

He shook his head slowly. "Not any more. Used to, when there weren't any fences, no taxes to pay – when they ran their beef on public lands – the big beef barons of the early days. That's when the fortunes were made in cattle. Not any more."

"But Charley Sargent? Surely he makes money with his race horses?"

"Now and then a killing perhaps. A lucky break. But by and large, he's spending money, not making it. He inherited his money. Now he's spending it the way he likes the best – raising race horses."

"What about sheep?"

"There's money in sheep, if you have the right sort of land for it. In the good years, that is, and when the market is right. But it's a big gamble. You can make a lot, and you lose a lot. The ranchers that are raising sheep now – they're a new bunch. Came in with fresh capital. I met Summerville in the Stockgrowers' Bank – we got to talking – he said nobody in Wyoming makes money any more except the Dude ranchers. And *he knows*," added Rob grimly.

"Then why – why – " said Nell, and hesitated to finish her sentence. Again she felt the panic rising.

"Why are we here, trying it?" said Rob. "Well I still think horses are the best bet."

Like Kennie, thought Nell. One idea in his head, and he'll never give up –

"A well-bred, well-trained registered four-year-old horse is worth at least twice as much as a prime steer – perhaps four times as much. It's true that a horse eats twice as much; on the same piece of land you can only run half as many horses, but – if there were decent markets for highbred stuff – you might make money. Trouble is, the markets."

"The Army seems the only sure market – "

"Sure; but they don't pay enough. At the Army Remount Depots, it costs them nearly a thousand dollars to raise a colt to four years. They pay us ranchers one hundred and fifty, or one hundred and seventy-five. You can't even get back the cost of production at that figure."

"Polo – "

"Polo's the only hope. For a well-trained polo pony you can get anywhere from two hundred to two thousand. But you've got to sell them as individuals – under the saddle, not in carloads. And I haven't any connection – no one to show them and promote sales."

"When the boys grow up – "

"That's it. Howard and Ken. With the start they've got, they'll be crack riders, they can be polo players – show and sell – and then, Nell –"

Rob turned his eyes to her. They had such burning intensity, she almost expected to see them glow in the dark, like cats' eyes.

She gathered up her sewing to put it away, and the little brown cat, squeezed down by her side in the arm chair, moved, stretched and turned over on her back, mewing.

"What's your hurry?" asked Rob.

"I've finished my mending."

"Stick around. I've just got a little more to go over here." He laid down his pipe, picked up his pencil again, and Nell leaned back in her chair.

Pauly, on her back, closed her eyes. Nell's hand sank into the soft cream-coloured fur on her belly.

Nell began to fall asleep. She was going down, floating deeper. Delicious – She roused herself with an effort.

Rob put out his hand and clasped her arm. "Don't go."

"I'll be asleep if I don't. And I've got to set the sponge for tomorrow's baking."

"I wish you wouldn't bake. Do as all the other country people do. Eat out of cans. Buy your bread at the Safeway in town."

"That stuff! Made of sawdust blown up – no taste – you could blow it across the room."

"I don't want you to work so hard."

"It isn't much. The boys love it."

"And so do I."

"And I do myself."

"But you do too much. Bad enough for me to be slaving – not you – "

Nell got up and Pauly hit the floor with a little grunt. "You come in when you've finished."

She went into the kitchen where one kerosene lamp was still burning, hung on the wall by the big black coal stove.

Rob finished his figures, closed his book, put it away and leaned his head on his hand, tapping with his pencil absent-mindedly on the blotter. He had caught a frightened look on Nell's face, when she was sitting there sewing, and it haunted him. And I didn't tell her the half of it, he thought. I shouldn't ever have done it. What a life for her. Damned if I won't quit. I quit the Army. Now the ranch. . . . No. Not licked yet, not by a damned sight. Boys growing up . . . Howard's a help already. Ken . . . Ken . . . now what am I going to do with that little son of a gun? Could have shaken the teeth out of his head today. Never can be where he ought to be, run an errand and get back on time, do a little job right, or remember what he's told. Give him a colt, Nell said. Give him a colt because he damn near stampeded the whole brood mare bunch over the Rock Slide. It it hadn't been for Banner – Great Guns! What a horse. Ahead of me all the time. If he passes it on to the colts, that kind of head work, and the heart and the courage, what polo ponies I'll have. That's one thing that's gone right. The blood in my horses . . . all but the Albino strain. That loco brute Rocket – always out in front with her nose in the air looking for trouble, and the three others. She's the worst. Not one of 'em really broke. I ought to shoot 'em all. I would, too, if they weren't so damned fast. Now I wonder what she meant by that give him a colt. I'd like to. Got to get closer to the kid some way. Every time I'm all set for a get-together session with him he hands me a facer like this thing he pulled today. I want to give him a colt and he makes me give him a bawling out. He doesn't mean it. Wants to please me, I can see that. Looks to me sometimes as if he was afraid of me. Don't like the way he turns his head away and looks down. Never comes to me for help. That's bad. He ought to turn to me . . . my fault somehow . . . or else he's just at an impossible age . . . but Howard wasn't . . . got to get friends with him . . . maybe this summer . . .

Rob got wearily and stiffly to his feet, stood in thought a moment, then put out the gasoline desk lamp and walked into the living room.

He called through the dining room to Nell, "I'll be there in a minute – don't go away – I've got to go up to the bunk house," and went out the front door and turned to the right.

Overhead the sky was clear, but in the southwest the heavy bank of clouds was spreading. Unless the wind rose again and scattered it, they'd have a storm.

As McLaughlin approached the bunk house he could see light burning inside. He pushed open the door with a clatter and crossed the dark kitchen to the living room. Here, Gus and Tim were seated at the long table, on which burned two kerosene lamps.

Gus was mending a bridle; Tim was drawing a picture, copying from a poster propped on the table. Before him was a bottle of India ink and in his hand a drawing pen. Tim's ambition was to be a sign-painter. The picture was of a voluptuous-hipped young woman, sitting on the end of a bench, looking coyly sideways at a youth on the other end. The room was already lavishly decorated with Tim's drawings, all of them, apparently, images of the same seductive female in different poses.

"Hello boys."

"Hello, Boss."

"I was just thinking," McLaughlin paused. His eyes were fixed absently on Tim's face, which was a rich dark colour, from dirt or sunburn or both, and wore its habitual expression of comic mystification. Tim was always expecting a laugh, but never knew why.

"What's that bridle, Gus?"

"De one Ken busted dis mornin'," said the Swede.

"I left Rocket in the Stable Pasture. She broke away from the gang just there at the gate to the County Road — raced along the fence hell for leather. The rest of them were going through nicely and for once none of them followed her and she was out of sight in a minute."

"Dot mare!"

"I closed the gate and went on with the bunch. Left her inside. It's just as well. I've got to get her into the chute and get that noose of rope off her neck, or she'll hang herself one of these days – I can do that tomorrow and then put her out and she'll find her way up to the bunch alone. See that the gates into the Home Pasture and the corrals are kept closed. I don't want her to get out. Where's the mare Ken was riding this morning?"

"Cigarette? I caught her up and put her into the Home Pasture," said Tim. "Thought Ken would be wantin' her agin."

"That's all right then. Good night, boys."

Rob went back to the house. Nell was still in the kitchen. He sat down in the corner at the table, and took out his pipe.

"Well – what about Ken and the colt?"

Nell wet a clean cloth at the faucet, wrung it out, folded it in a big square, laid it over the yellow bowl with the sponge and set the bowl on top of the warming oven. Then she seated herself on the edge of the table, clasped one knee and looked at Rob.

"I want you to give him a colt."

"He doesn't deserve one."

"What's that got to do with it? Aren't you ever going to give him a colt?"

"Sure I am. I've been expecting to."

"Well, why don't you then?"

"I told you – he doesn't deserve it."

"But Rob, he never will."

"Why won't he? Howard did."

"Ken's different. He's so far behind now, it's hopeless If you wait until he catches up, and he really has it coming to him, he just won't get one at all."

Rob ruminated. "If he attends to his studies this summer – "

"That's another thing, Rob. That isn't going to get anywhere."

Rob's expression of shock and consternation was almost comical. "Not going to get anywhere! For God's sake! That's what I'm counting on – why won't he?"

54

"He really can't study. He hasn't the habit."

"Didn't he study today?"

Nell laughed. "He exposed himself to his books – "

Rob got up and walked up and down the floor. "But my God – I've told him to. I've given the order – "

Nell kept discreetly quiet. Of all the manoeuvres that were difficult for Rob, a right about face was the most difficult.

After a while she said, "Let's try a different method. Ken needs to succeed at something. Howard's too far ahead of him. Bigger and smarter and his wits about him, and – "

"Ken doesn't half try; doesn't stick at anything."

"But he's crazy for a colt of his own. He can't think of another thing."

"But Nell, it's all backwards. You can't bribe children to do their duty."

"Not a bribe – " she hesitated.

"No? What would you call it?"

She tried to think it out. "I just have the feeling Ken isn't going to pull anything off." She looked across at Rob. "And it's time he did. It isn't the school marks alone, but I just don't want things to go on any longer with Ken never coming out at the right end of anything."

"I'm beginning to think he's just dumb."

"He's not dumb – "

"This thing he pulled today – stampeding the mares – "

"You know he didn't mean to – "

"That's just the point. It's stupidity and carelessness. Nothing I say to him makes any impression. He still goes around wool-gathering, not knowing where he is or what's going on around him."

"Maybe a little thing like this would turn the trick. If he had a colt of his own, trained him, rode him –"

"But it isn't a little thing. It's not easy to break and school a colt the way Howard has schooled Highboy.

I'm not going to have a good horse spoiled by Ken's careless ways. He never knows what he's doing."

"If Ken could really accomplish something like this, it would make a big difference in him."

"That's a big *if*."

"Rob, it's important. He's got to get square somehow. The way he looked tonight. Hang-dog – sullen almost. He's in everybody's bad graces. What he needs really is – "

"To snap out of it."

"Well, if you want to put it that way. I was going to say he needs to grow up a little."

"How will having a colt make him grow up?"

"Well, *you* know, something of his own. Responsibility. You see, he'd have something real, in flesh and blood, that he cared about more than all the things he goes mooning about. If he achieves anything with the colt, I think it'll show in everything he does next year. He'll be more of a man."

She took off her apron.

They put out the kitchen lamp, went down the step into the living-room and Rob called, "Here Kim, here Chaps!"

Reluctantly the dogs rose from their mats, stretching themselves; yawned, and followed Rob and Nell out on to the terrace.

Four dark horse shapes took fright and leaped away from the fountain, galloped off a little, then turned and stood, watching curiously.

Rob and Nell led the dogs away around the corner of the house and put them into the tool shed. Returning, they sat down on the coping of the fountain.

The horses were coming back, a few steps at a time, their ears pricked.

"Which are they?" asked Nell.

"The three-year-old broncs."

Nell said nothing. The fact that they had been left here,

56

in the Home Pasture, which was just a ring of barbed wire fence about a half mile in area, enclosing a section of woods, hills and fields around the ranch buildings, meant that they were at hand for use. He was going to break them. "But not if I know anything about it," said Nell to herself.

"Four of the mares haven't foaled yet. I think Rocket's dry this year," Rob said.

"I thought Rocket had foaled already. A black horse colt. The other day when I was down in the meadow, there was a black horse colt that I thought was hers. A little new one."

"I thought so too. But when she made that break away from the bunch today there was no colt following her."

"But I saw it nursing – "

"Must have been nursing on one of the other black mares. This time of year, when their coats are so rough, it's hard to tell them apart."

"Rob, I'm sure it was Rocket – "

Rob suddenly got to his feet. Nell knew the thought of a colt left down there in Castle Rock meadow, perhaps hidden somewhere in the aspen grove the far end, perhaps hurt – would worry him.

"But I rode all through the aspen grove," he said. "I didn't leave any colts behind. Besides, if she'd had a colt, Rocket wouldn't have left it. You never can get her away from her colts."

He sat down again on the coping and watched the horses that were coming towards him, step by step. "I'll drive down to the meadow tomorrow and take another look."

The four horses kept their eyes fixed upon him. They knew him. The smell of him, the look of him. At the sound of his voice, if it came from half a mile away, every horse on the ranch stopped in his tracks and looked around. They stood in a half circle in the moonlight facing him.

"They want oats," said Rob. "I haven't got any oats, you beggars!" He raised his arms, flapped them, yelling, and the horses leaped and galloped away into the darkness.

Rob and Nell laughed.

The moon was well up, huge and theatrical above the black pine branches on the hill. The Green was in shadow, just the tips of the cottonwoods catching the light. They sat in silence, watching the moon climb. More and more of the cottonwoods rose into the light, floating softly.

"They're like ballet girls," said Nell, "dancing on the Green."

The horses were returning. Very slowly they came close, and made a ring, watching Rob.

In the bunk house Gus yawned and put away his work.

"Give us a tune, Tim, while I finish my pipe. Den I'm turnin' in."

Tim wound the little gramophone, inspected the records carefully, chose one and put it on.

Seated again, his chair tilted against the wall, Tim leaned his head back and both men were silent.

The tune spun out on the clear night air, and reached Rob and Nell sitting on the coping of the fountain.

It was an old song, with all the childish pathos of the melodies that are loved on the plains, or born there; and seemed to come from a voice singing far away.

> Dar-ar-ar-ling I am growing o-o-old,
> Sil-il-ver thrads among the go-o-old,
> Shine upon my brow today-ay-ay,
> Life is fading fa-a-ast away.

The song ended.

Gus sighed. The needle spun round and round, finally grinding on the record, and Tim got up and turned it off.

Chapter Six

The mile-square Stable Pasture, so called because it was nearest to the stables, was a terrain of startling wildness and beauty. A broad runway of level grass went along the County Road fence on the south. North and west, it ran into low hills, with a sparse, erratic growth of large twisted pines, and the soil here was a shallow layer over a mountain crag which broke through everywhere in cliffs and sharp stone teeth. Out of the rock-clefts grew pines and junipers. At the base of the cliffs were caverns in which were skeletons and piles of bones, remnants of wild animal orgies. The cliffs overhung fragrant little dells where mushrooms and larkspur and strawberry plants pushed up through the loam and pine needles. Going north, the hills and cliffs became steeper; and at last, in a series of broken, wooded steppes, plunged down to the level of

59

Deercreek, the mountain stream which formed the northern boundary.

The Stable Pasture was an endless field of exploration for Howard and Ken. Just to find a new path up or down the Steppes, without getting pocketed somewhere from which there was hardly a way out, was a day's delight. Nell loved to wander in it, or to take a book with her for a whole afternoon in some small secret dell. Here, all summer long, the mysterious shapes of the deer stole like shadows across the shafts of sunlight. One couldn't sit very long, quiet and still and watching, without seeing the slow determined movement of a porcupine, or the serpentine undulations of a pretty, white-striped skunk, or the awkward plunges and playful tumbling dashes of whistling pigs, or the continuous soft movement of gophers, cottontails and jacks. If there was no meat for dinner, Nell or either of the boys could take a twenty-two and spend an hour in the Stable Pasture in the late afternoon and bring home a half dozen tender young cottontails.

That night Rocket had the pasture all to herself. She had made the rounds of it several times.

She stood now at the closed gate which opened on the County Road and looked across at the grassy slopes of the Saddle Back. They shone a bright silvery grey under the moon. Suddenly she lifted her hind leg like a dog, swung her head savagely around and tried to butt her bag. It was hot and bursting. She turned again and stood motionless, looking up at the range, her ears pricked.

She started off on a fast trot along the fence. With long thrusting strides she made the ground run away from her. Her big haunches crinkled with each piston stroke; her head was high, nose reaching up, her sparse irregular mane fell untidily, part on one side, part on the other side of her neck. The frayed piece of lariat was knotted about her neck and hung under the mane. A fine line of white ringed each eye. She had an angry, crazy look.

60

She stopped at the corner of the pasture where another barbed-wire fence came in at right angles. Standing there, throwing a far, piercing gaze into the distance, her ears moving incessantly, she trembled to every sound that drifted on the still air. Suddenly she started off again, following the cross fence.

All in through the rough and varied terrain of the Pasture ran threads of paths. Rob had found a way down to Deercreek for the automobile. The horses knew it from birth and covered it all, clawing their way up, leaping from ledge to ledge, sliding down on their haunches, sure-footed as mountain goats.

For an hour Rocket scoured the pasture, crashing down the Steppes to Deercreek, forcing her way through the thicket on the other side of the stream, standing at the northern fence, sniffing.

Far over yonder were the hay meadows. Castle Rock Meadow farthest of all.

It was the breeze that played over Castle Rock Meadow, the aspen grove at the far end, that she wanted to smell.

But for all her searching and listening, there was no little whimper for her ears, nor the touch of fumbling warm tongue and lips upon her bag, nor the closeness of a nimble little shape running at her side.

After a moment or two she continued her way along the fence, going at a long swinging trot; then turned another corner and began to climb and finally had made the complete round of the boundaries of the pasture once more.

She came out of the pines, cantered down the hill, went past the stables and pulled up at the County Road fence. Standing here she sent a loud ringing neigh into the night, hurling it like a fierce accusation.

A mile or more away on the Saddle Back, Banner heard the neigh and pricked his ears. He appeared to appraise the importance of it, dismiss it as making no immediate demands upon him and swung his head back again.

61

The cry was heard, too, by the band of yearlings grazing quietly on the other side of the crest. A little golden filly, who might have been Banner in miniature, raised her head sharply and stood alert, listening.

The loud angry neigh came again, and the sorrel filly neighed in reply and flung herself into a gallop. On the crest of the hill she stood, looking down at the County Road and the Stable Pasture.

Rocket's head was lifted and her ears strained forward. She had heard the whinny of the little sorrel, and a shuddering took her. She began to prance up and down inside the fence, then turned and galloped away from it, in the direction of Castle Rock. She had cried for her foal — there had been an answer, and one that touched her maternity, but still, not the voice of the little one who so lately had been part of herself; and she was confused, and in bewilderment galloped toward the dark woods that lay between her and Castle Rock.

The yearling filly neighed again and plunged down the hill toward the road. The voice tore at Rocket. She stopped; turned; an answering neigh broke from her; and suddenly, indecision left her, and she reversed her direction and galloped toward the fence.

Very few untrained horses are jumpers, and a western mustang will always break through a wire fence rather than leap it, but the joy and eagerness in Rocket's heart gave her wings, and she made a beautiful clean jump over the wires and the two horses rushed to each other, pressed their cheeks together, intertwined their heads and necks, with loving, excited whinnies.

Rocket wanted more. Her bursting bag — this colt, as well as the little one she had lost, surely this yearling child of hers could take the milk that was causing her agony.

Her voice coaxed. She turned herself in the proper position to the little sorrel and whinnied again. But the yearling had been on grass for six months; the instinct to nurse was dead. It stood, unresponsive, head turned back toward the hill, where now it heard its comrades running.

Rocket whinnied again in desperation. She swung her haunches close against the colt. The youngster answered with a sensitive and affectionate neigh, and turned to rest its head on top of the mare's haunches. Rocket moved closer, the golden head slipped down and sideways, at last it was there, reaching under, fumbling for the teat. Rocket stood motionless, her head turned over the haunch of the nursing yearling.

An hour later, the black mare and the golden yearling were cantering side by side; they had left the ranch and the Saddle Back far behind them. Ahead of them were the broken headlands of the Colorado border, and in their nostrils the smell of the snow from the faraway mountains of the Neversummer Range.

Chapter Seven

Even before he opened his eyes next morning Ken knew that something was wrong, and he pushed away the moment of complete awakening. He lay facing the window and saw that the pines on the hill were quiet. No wind today.

Then he remembered. He had stampeded the mares.

He had a feeling that it was late. For some time he had been half hearing all the early morning noises. Gus opening the kitchen door. The only reason his steps across the kitchen floor and the shaking down of the ashes and the making of the fire didn't wake everyone was because they were so used to it. There had been steps going down, too, and his mother's voice saying, Time to get up, boys –

He slipped out of bed and went to the window, hitching up his pyjamas. Howard was on the terrace right underneath, and Ken could see the top of his head, black and smooth, with the part exactly in the centre. He had on blue jeans, and a clean chambray shirt and a red bandana.

Howard looked up. "Hi."

Ken stared at him without answering.

Howard's black eyebrows and his thin mouth were straight lines across his face. He was smiling a little but his eyes were watching craftily.

"Mad at me, ain't you?"

"Tattletale!"

"I didn't tell on you."

"Yer a liar."

"All I did was ask if Cigarette tossed you, and if you found the blanket."

"You started it – you knew I'd get it in the neck –"

"That's not lying."

"Yer always gettin' me in trouble – you want to – "

"Say, let's make up, Ken – we could go down to the swimmin' pool – it's gonna be hot."

Ken glowered.

"We could start on the colts – "

"What colts?"

"Our summer colts. Dad left four of 'em in the Calf Pasture yesterday. We gotta halter-break them, like we did last year. I get first choice he said."

"Do you choose one and then I choose one and then you and then I? Or do you choose both yours first?"

"Well he said I could choose both first – "

"I betcher lyin' – "

"Tell you what, Ken, if you'll make up, I'll choose just one and let you choose next."

Their father's voice came loudly, "Didn't I tell you to watch that sprinkler, Howard?"

Howard hastily changed the sprinkler.

McLaughlin was coming from the tool house. He had let out the dogs and they were jumping around him frantic with joy, as if they were afraid, every night, there would never be another letting out or another morning.

McLaughlin had a shovel in his hand and went about

the Green cleaning it of the manure the horses had left and shouting to Howard about taking an interest in the grass that had been so hard to start and was still hard to keep green.

The red Rhode Island hen that had stolen a nest followed him, clucking and picking at the manure spots, and the hatch of cheeping yellow chicks swarmed around her, tiny feet twinkling at her call, and wing-fluffs beating the air.

Ken faded back into the room and hastily began to dress.

The smell of coffee filled the house.

Howard watched his sprinkler, moving it, little by little, down the terrace, and planned his day. Ken would be all right now, he thought, he was never hard to manage – they might have fun in the swimming pool – or go shooting –

"Breakfast!" sang out Nell's voice. She ran out on to the terrace She had on a green dress with a zipper all the way down the front and a sash across the back. She clapped her hands and yelled for them to come, and Rob dropped his shovel and ran at her, and Ken stopped tying his necktie to watch. His mouth was open and there was a smile on his face because it was always fun when his father and mother started playing. She dodged and ran around the fountain, and her husband chased her and reached out a hand and caught her sash and undid it, and she screamed and ran for the steps, and both dogs ran in between them barking and almost tripped him up.

They'd gone in. Ken hurried to finish but he hated to go down, he felt so out of things. On the way downstairs he stopped before the picture of the duck. It was a big black duck with white breast and legs and white bars on his wings. He was fierce and handsome standing on his rock, just about to launch himself into the waves of the grey, choppy lake. There was such a reaching in his eager beak and one lifted foot and the forward tilt of his body, Ken felt as if it dragged him in too. In another second he would feel the icy sting and shock of the water, the bitter cold, sharp, up-pricked waves, and the greyness of the misty air hanging over it, full of fear and loneliness. His skin went gooseflesh.

At the breakfast table his father was waiting to hear Ken clatter the rest of the way downstairs.

"I bet he's looking at the duck," said Howard.

"What duck?"

"On the landing. He looks at it for an hour sometimes."

"Howard," reproved Nell, "he never looks at it for an hour."

"Well, a long time – seems like an hour."

"In God's name!" McLaughlin's voice was rising. "What duck on the landing?"

"My Audubon print," explained Nell quickly. "The one that hangs under the clock. Ken likes to look at it."

"Ken!" roared his father; and hastily Ken's sturdy shoes clattered the rest of the way down the stairs, and he came into the kitchen, his hair meticulously parted and slicked down, and his face sullen.

"What did you stop on the landing for?"

Ken opened his napkin and looked down, embarrassed. "I was looking at the duck."

"The duck! Out the window?"

"The duck in the picture there."

There was a little amused glint in Nell's eyes as she helped Ken to oatmeal.

"Didn't you know we were at breakfast?"

"I – I – "

"Didn't think," finished his father for him.

Ken didn't look up or make any reply. He had known it would be like this. He poured cream on his oatmeal and reached for the brown sugar.

"Ken," said his father, "I'm going to take back an order I gave you yesterday. I'm going to remit your hour of study."

66

Ken looked at his father in astonishment – his mouth opening in relief and pleasure.

"I've got other plans for you this summer," McLaughlin continued pompously, and Nell tucked her face down to hide her smile. How often had she heard Rob order a baulky horse to *Whoo!* or seen him spur and lash a runaway!

"And," continued Rob blandly, "I'm going to give you a colt."

Ken shot out of his chair. Spoon and dishes went clattering.

"A – a – spring colt, Dad? Or a yearling?"

McLaughlin was taken aback, but Nell dropped her eyes again. If Ken got a yearling colt, he'd be even up with Howard.

"A yearling colt, your father means, Kennie," she said smoothly. "Sit down and eat your breakfast – look what you've done to your porridge."

Ken gathered up the china and silver he had scattered, replaced them and sat down again. Colour had rushed to his face.

"I'll give it to you a week from today," said his father. "Between now and then you can look them over and make your choice."

"I can have any yearling colt on the ranch that I want?" asked Ken.

His father nodded calmly, pushed his chair back and took out his pipe.

Speechless, Ken turned to look at Howard and the two boys eyed each other.

Even up, at last.

"Does it have to be a yearling colt, Dad?" asked Howard. Could it be a spring colt if he'd rather have a spring colt?"

"It could be anything foaled on the ranch since a year ago," said McLaughlin. "There are eighteen yearlings.

So far, thirteen or fourteen new colts; a few to come yet."

"Will you take a yearling or a spring colt, Ken?" asked Howard.

In answer, Ken turned upon Howard an exaggerated pitying sneer, copied from the movies, and mastered only after much practice.

But his father asked the same thing. "Yearling or spring colt, Ken?"

Ken answered, "A yearling."

"Horse or filly?"

This stopped him. His eyes lost focus as mental images crowded. Rocket was a mare. But there was Banner. And the Albino, mustang hero. There emerged from the confusion a definite sense of the superiority of the male.

"I'll take a horse colt." His voice was final and authoritative. An imperceptible glance passed between Nell and her husband.

McLaughlin said, "That narrows it down. Let's see – how many horse colts were foaled last year?"

"Ten fillies and eight horse colts," said Howard. "You've got eight horse colts to choose from, Ken."

Things were moving very fast for Ken, horses crowding him –

"Which were they?" said Nell. "I've got them all down in the Stud Book. I left it up at the stables the other day, in the tack room. Ken, run up and get it, and we'll look over the list."

"I'll go too," said Howard, sliding out of his chair; and both boys rushed out the door.

Ken tore ahead. A colt – a colt! His own!

His mind was full of images. A little foal just born, almost knocked down by its mother's tongue licking it . . . Banner rearing, his great forefeet beating the air, his big light belly, his fierce face and arching neck – a little yearling running . . . a black . . . a chestnut . . . his colt was all of them . . .

He dropped his head back and yelled; he pranced and galloped.

Howard caught up with him and said, "You crazy!"

"My colt, my colt," sang Ken. He ran in a circle pacing, racking. He stuck his elbows out, said, "Whoa, there! Hi!" He tossed his head and shook his mane.

"You goofy!" exclaimed Howard, watching him.

Ken rushed at him with fists up. Howard fell into position and they sparred. Ken didn't care what happened to him. His arms went like flails. Howard blocked his blows easily.

Ken broke out of it and went flying up to the stable. He had a sharp consciousness of change and new importance. Things had begun at last. Things could be real now.

They found the Stud Book and ran back with it.

As Nell read out the list of yearlings and the names of their dams Ken began to feel queer. These were definite flesh and blood animals; named, described, tagged, in a book; not the colts that had kicked their heels and played and tossed their manes in his dreams. He felt the sense of loss which every dreamer feels when the dream moves up, comes close, and at last is concrete.

"I haven't named them all," Nell was saying. "There were some I never saw. They had run off somewhere when I went up on Twenty to look them over and put them in the book."

"The bronc bunch," grunted McLaughlin, referring to the progeny of the Albino. "They're always missing when they're wanted."

"Ken and I trained four of these yearlings ourselves," said Howard.

Every summer the two boys had the job of handling and halter-breaking four of the spring colts.

"The colts the boys trained last summer were Doughboy and College Boy and Lassie and Firefly," said Nell, studying the book. "Two horse colts and two fillies."

"Say, Ken," said Howard eagerly, "why don't you

69

take Doughboy? He was one of yours. And when he grows up he'll be sort of twins with mine, in his name anyway. Doughboy, Highboy, see?"

But Ken looked scornful. Doughboy would never have half Highboy's speed. Last summer McLaughlin, looking over the colts, had said, "He's a chunk. We'll name him Doughboy. He might turn out a heavy hunter. Look at the big legs on him!"

"Lassie then," suggested Howard again. "If you want speed. She's fast as anything, and she's black as ink. Like Highboy."

"I said I was going to take a *horse*," said Ken. "Besides, Dad said Lassie'll never go over fifteen hands."

"Remember one thing, Ken," said McLaughlin. "You can't tell much about a colt when it's new-born, and not always much more when it's a yearling. Blood's the thing. The prepotency of blood – "

They had heard this term often, for whenever McLaughlin got talking about horses he used it.

"That's the trouble with this stuff I've got from the Albino. He had prepotency. That devil passed on his traits. They don't wear out. Must have had some magnificent blood strains somewhere in his ancestry. Arab probably. Put enough Arab blood into a line and it gives prepotency – to the traits you don't want as well as to those you do. Lots of Arab blood in these western mustangs. Comes from the Arab and Barb horses the Spaniards brought over – " McLaughlin got up, went to the shelf beside the spice closet, and took down one his favourite books on the genealogy of the American horse. He turned the pages, looking for a passage.

Chapter Eight

At dinner, McLaughlin said the first thing he was going to do was to get Rocket into the corrals, and into the chute, cut the piece of rope off her neck, then drive her out of the Stable Pasture and out on to the range with the other brood mares.

"Until I get that done," said he, "I can't turn the gelded colts into the Stable Pasture – she'd get mixed up with them and I'd have the hell of a time cutting her out again."

"How long will you keep the colts in the Stable Pasture?" asked Nell.

"About a week. I've got to keep my eye on them. They'll have to be exercised daily. After that, they can go out on to the range with the others. You boys can give them a hard run every day. Ride 'em like hell. This is your chance to whoop it up and yell and act like cowboys."

"Why?" asked Howard.

"If there should be an infected one amongst them — which is always possible — he'd just stand around until he dies. Make him run. That causes drainage of the wound, stirs up circulation. If they're left alone, they'll stand around and mope and won't eat enough to keep up their strength."

Ken hadn't wanted his dinner. Even the smell of the food tightened the flesh at the base of his nostrils.

Nell was looking at him. She said, "You can leave the table if you want, Ken. Put up my hammock for me. I may want it later."

Ken went out to the terrace. Over one part was a lattice roof, made of aspen poles. It had been built to hold a canvas and make shade against the hot summer sun. To Nell it was the Pergola, and she was training vines to run up the corner poles. Someday they would grow all over the lattice and make shade enough without any canvas, and the sunlight would filter through, and the green leaves would hang down, and underneath it would be a cool green and gold light.

Ken stood looking up. The canvas had not yet been spread and the direct glaring light hurt his eyes.

Ken got the hammock, hung it near the Pergola and lay down in it on his back, with feet and hands dangling over the sides, giving little shoves against the ground.

The lilac bushes in the angle near the stone steps and the flowers of the border gave off a strong fragrance in the heat. There were horses on the Green, some of them drinking at the fountain, some cropping the grass, some just standing looking at the house. There were no stallions there, just mares and geldings.

Nell came out with her apron tied around her and her coffee cup in her hand and stood looking at the sky.

"Golly, it's hot!" she said. "It's time we had the canvas up."

She looked over at Ken, as she stood stirring her coffee,

and then sat down in one of the hickory chairs beside him.

He turned his face to her, beginning to smile; and she put out her hand and pushed the damp hair back from his forehead.

"I really do feel an awful lot different, Mother," he said. "When I got up this morning and didn't even know I was going to have a colt seems awful far away."

People grow up that way," said Nell. "In spurts. All of a sudden, they are years older."

Ken's face became thoughtful. "Besides, I can have a filly instead of a horse colt. Dad rides a mare."

McLaughlin's voice, laughing loudly, came out the kitchen window, and the horses on the Green raised their heads, looked at the house and walked expectantly towards it.

McLaughlin appeared in the doorway. "Look at the beggars. Beggin' for oats – "

He disappeared again. There was always a bucket of oats hanging on a hook in the enclosed porch outside the kitchen door. He came out with the bucket and went down on the Green to the horses. They crowded around him.

On such occasions he insisted on their good behaviour. This meant observance of rules of fair play and turn about. A horse that stuck his nose into the bucket and would not take it out would get a good smack on the side of the head. If they whirled and lashed each other in their jealousy and greediness, he put the bucket behind him and delivered a lecture, the tone of his voice expressing such surprise and indignation that they would hang their heads and all but promise never to do it again. Sometimes he would be completely surrounded and hidden and a scrimmage would start. Big bodies wheeling, rearing, heels lashing this way and that, hoofs pawing the air. One would think he must be down and trampled. But always he would emerge, swinging the bucket in one hand, smacking the nose of this or that horse angrily with the back of the other hand, his voice rising in harsh reprimand. And gradually the horses would calm down again and follow him meekly.

"Ken," said his father, "run down and open the gate into the Calf Pasture. I left the four foals with their dams in there yesterday. The ones that you and Howard are to halter-break this summer. Let them come in here with the bunch."

Ken ran down the Green to the gate beside the corral of the cow barn, which opened into the Calf Pasture, and hooked it back, but no mares were in sight.

Rob gave his trilling whistle which, standing close beside him, you could hardly hear, but which carried a great distance.

Presently there appeared the sharp head of a horse around the shoulder of the hill which was at the upper end of the pasture. Then another and another. Three little colts came out with their free dancing steps – as if they had springs under their hoofs. Soon all four mares with their foals were trotting towards the gate. They slowed up as they came through and walked slowly on to the Green.

"Oh, look at Highboy and Tango!" exclaimed Nell.

Highboy, who had wandered some distance away and was nosing for clover on the side of the hill, had suddenly spied the mares, and something had excited him.

A pretty black mare was looking at him, standing in a pose of excited recognition.

Then with loud neighs, the two rushed towards each other, and when they met, they touched their faces, pressed their cheeks together, and at last Highboy rose lightly, standing close beside her, and flung one foreleg over her neck.

Nell and Rob and the boys were laughing.

"Reunion," said Rob. "They were born the same spring and have always been sweethearts, and they were separated all through the winter while I had the mares down in the meadow."

74

Nell said, "Exactly the way I used to be with my best little girl friend when we'd been away from each other for the summer."

"The most affectionate animal in the world," said Rob. "You don't see the young ones leaving their mothers if they can help it. They stay in the family group. You'll often see a mare on the plains with a four-year-old colt, and a three-year-old, and a two, and a one, and a foal. All together. They don't break up unless something happens to make them. And they never forget."

Highboy and Tango wandered away together. Tango's little black colt, about a month old, following and trying to nurse.

"It's her first colt," said Rob. "Looks like a good one. Howard, hand me the bucket. This is a good chance to give the colts their initiation."

He fed the mares first and then offered it to the colts.

They would have been terrified, but seeing that their mothers were enjoying it, they nosed the bucket, gave it a sniff, and, hating the metal and the human smell of the hand, wheeled and pranced off. At a safe distance they turned, stood watching, and at last edged up again.

Rob never missed a chance to instruct the boys in horse psychology and the right approach to training.

"This is the beginning," he said, "of their getting used to human beings. It would have been better to start with these little fellows when they were just a few days old, as soon as they got their legs, and started out on their careers of being horses. They've been alone and free down in the meadow since they were born a few weeks ago, and that's time lost. Worse than lost, for they learned a world in which there are no human beings – just horses, grass, running water, trees, perhaps the strangeness of a wooden fence post and a wire fence – nothing more. And now they've got to change their minds about the world. It's different from what they've learned. It's a world where humans take the first place. Human beings master them.

They have to obey. Humans are the most important of all. But they'll soon learn."

"They're learning already," said Howard. "You can see them."

"They learn from their mothers. They copy. They do everything their mothers do. That's why it's practically impossible to raise a good-tempered colt from a bad tempered mare. That's why I never have any luck with the colts of the wild mares I get. The colts are corrupted from birth – just as wild as their mothers. You can't train it out of them."

The light changed suddenly, and McLaughlin looked at the sky. The heavy cloud bank in the southwest had engulfed the sun and a coolness came into the air.

"It's going to rain," he said. "Will you ride this afternoon, Nell?"

"Later," she answered. "I've got to bake my bread now before the fire goes down."

"I'm going for the mail – anything you want?"

"Two cakes of Fleischman's yeast, and Gus wanted tobacco – Rough Cut – the next time anyone went to the store."

She went back into the house and the boys ran to the big red Studebaker, where it stood on the hill behind the house. Howard got in the front seat, and Ken in the back.

Just about to let in the clutch, McLaughlin paused and looked at Howard.

"By the way, Howard, when did you ride Highboy last?"

"Yesterday afternoon."

"I was noticing his legs – you turned him out with dirty legs."

"I groomed him," Howard wriggled.

"Yes, down to his knees."

"He kicks."

"And whose fault is that?"

Howard sat in silence.

"This would be a good time," said McLaughlin, "to take him up to the stables and groom him. He's right there where you can easily catch him."

"Can't I go with you to the store first?" asked Howard.

McLaughlin sat looking around at the weather signs, as if he had not heard.

Just like his father to wait until a little fun was up and then choose that time to make him groom Highboy.

He got out slowly. Ken climbed into the front seat.

"Take out the stone from in front of the wheel," said his father.

Howard obeyed and the car slid down the hill, the gears gripped, the engine started, and it rattled over the cattle guard and was off down the stretch of straight gravel road over the little stone bridge that spanned Lone Tree Creek, on up and around the shoulder of the wooded hill, and out of sight.

Chapter Nine

There were two miles of winding road with a fine hard-packed surface of reddish decomposed granite; then a sharp turn under the big sign that said GOOSE BAR RANCH, and out on to the Lincoln Highway.

"Dad, I've decided to take a filly instead of a horse colt," said Ken.

McLaughlin laughed. "O.K. But don't take it too seriously, Ken."

Ken sat thinking about his colt. He had a week to choose. He would ride up to the Saddle Back every day, look over the yearlings –

"Something I want to say to you, Ken."

Ken looked up. The man-to-man way his father spoke to him made him feel they were almost friends already.

The car sped across the over-pass.

A train with two locomotives was passing underneath,

78

and when they reached the highway again, was running parallel with them. It whistled shrilly, the smoke drifted across the road and shut down on them like fog. McLaughlin didn't speak until they had passed the train and the smoke and noise had gone.

"It's this, Ken. I'm giving you a colt. Any colt you want. And yet, I'm not satisfied with the performance you've given this spring. You know that. Maybe you think it's funny I give you the colt when what you deserve – for flunking all your exams and pulling that stunt yesterday – is a good hiding."

Ken's face sobered, and he looked straight ahead.

McLaughlin continued. "I don't want you to think I'm letting you off. I'm not. I haven't gone soft – don't get that into your head. I expect just as much of you as I ever did. And this isn't any reward, because you haven't won a reward."

"What is it?"

"It's a partnership. I'm going to need the help of both of you boys, and you have to be trained so you'll know how to give it. You're going to train the yearling. I'll give you a little help just with the first breaking, but you'll train her, and she'll train you. I want you to make a good pony out of her. I want her to make a man out of you. Get me?"

"Yes, sir." Ken looked up with a wide smile lighting his face.

"But that's not all," said his father. "You've got other duties. You can give some time to your colt – not all your time. You've got two of these foals to halter-break –"

"Yes, sir."

"You've got to help exercise four horses for the Rodeo; run the gelded colts every day for half an hour for this whole week; help with all the ranch work the way you always do. I don't want to find you welshing on work because you're off playing with your colt –"

79

"No, sir."

"This giving you the colt is a kind of bargain between us. I give you the colt, you give me more obedience, more efficiency, than you ever have in your life before. Is it a bargain?"

"Yes, sir."

McLaughlin slapped his hand on Ken's knee, and a flush coloured the boy's cheeks.

They were silent for a while and Ken's eyes drifted across the landscape, then came back to the wide highway that ran, he knew, from the Atlantic to the Pacific seaboard, three thousand miles of macadam road, nearly straight. Some of the western roads he had been on with his father were empty of traffic. They cut the plains, straight and flat, as far as the eye could see. The cars that used them went at top speed, boring like bees into the distance, only a few in a day. Sometimes for hours, perhaps whole days, the road was empty. But the Lincoln Highway was alive with traffic. Each of the cars they passed told its story, or a brief word from his father gave Ken the clue. The transcontinental traffic looked it. Big, expensive-looking cars, covered with dust, loaded with luggage so that the rear ends hung low, spieling along at eighty miles an hour, going somewhere fast, miles to eat up before nightfall. Tourists, perhaps from New York or Boston, headed for some Dude Ranch or National Park for a vacation. As they flashed by, you could see, inside, the heads of women and girls tied up in bright handkerchiefs.

They passed a big truck, loaded with straight pine poles.

"Poles from Pole mountain," said McLaughlin. "Somebody's building a barn."

"Do they buy the poles?"

"Pole Mountain is a Government Reserve. You can get the poles free but you have to cut them and transport them. It costs money to get a load."

There was some local traffic; second-hand cars in none too good shape, of nearby ranchers; a few big cars of business and professional men running from Cheyenne to Laramie; some hard-worked roadsters and sedans of travelling men; one long caravan – "snake" they called it – of new cars being hauled from the East for sale in California, saving railroad transportation costs by using the Lincoln Highway.

As they arrived at Tie Siding, there drew up from the opposite direction a sample of the type of conveyance which is to be seen on every mile of the western highways. It was a Ford sedan, bulging and sagging like an old washerwoman. The top of it was piled with mattresses, chairs, tables, bedding. The rear end was festooned with bundles and boxes tied on with knotted lengths of clothes line, an old rusty stove, half covered by a bed quilt, was roped to one fender. Humanity of all ages packed it from floor to roof, and poured out when the door opened. Their faces were dry and wind-beaten and strained. Girls and boys alike wore faded, soiled denim pants. The small children and the baby looked both sick and sad. Their eyes were drawn up, there were deep lines on each side of the colourless mouths. One small youngster was bawling, not with fret or anger, but with a persistent despair.

McLaughlin turned off his engine and they sat a moment, watching.

"Where are they going to?" asked Ken.

"Just moving on. Poor people trying to find a way to live. They try the towns, can't make the grade, think the country would be easier, manage to get a homestead, or buy some land from someone else who has failed –"

"How can they pay for it?"

"They don't – they promise to pay, or give a share of the crops – or maybe they rent. And, of course, they get the worst land with little or no water, impossible for anyone to make a success of. And then they fail there too, and move on. The country is dotted with rotting barns and houses. And the land, that was good grass land once, is ruined, ploughed up, the native grass killed."

"But won't it grow again?"

"In about ten years. It's a crime to break ground in this country of high winds. The Indians knew that and they found a better way. Early in the spring or after the seed had fallen in the fall, they'd burn the old grass. Then there'd be new grass springing up unchoked, and no top soil ploughed up to blow away like dust with the first dry summer."

Mrs. Olsen, wife of the man who ran the combination Post Office and store, came hurrying out in her neat white pants and jacket.

"Hello," she said cheerfully.

She had a trim, close-cropped black head, a great deal of rouge on her cheeks and lips, and a quiet, efficient way of going about things.

"I'll take two gallons," said the tall, oldish man who had climbed out of the sedan, and he stood over Mrs. Olsen as she put the hose into the tank and the petrol began to pour.

Others of the family scattered around both sides of the store to the rest rooms. Several of the children crossed the road to stand watching a pair of brown bears that were in a big cage of woven steel wire. Ken and his father got out of the car and went to the store, in which a number of men were making purchases or sitting about.

Other cars were stopping for petrol, and Mrs. Olsen came running in and out to make change.

A truck stopped, and the driver came in for tobacco, while Mrs. Olsen filled his tank.

"What's your load?" asked McLaughlin.

"Dead calves."

"Dead calves!" said everyone.

Olsen said, "From Morrison's place, north across the highway, I'll bet –"

"That's right."

82

"I heerd they wuz cartin' the dead calves away in truck-loads from his place – hundreds of 'em –"

"That's right."

"Sure tough luck for Morrison," said Olsen. "If he don't find a way of clearin' his herd of abortion, don't seem likely he can keep goin' –"

Ken went out and climbed up on the sides of the truck and looked down at the load of corpses; dark red bodies, white faces, good Hereford calves. They smelled pretty bad already.

The driver was getting back in.

Ken jumped down again and went back to the store.

"Government's takin' a hand in clearin' the state of abortion," said Crane, over in the corner of the store. "Specially dairy stock. But it's my guess if they forbid milk to be sold, over the whole country, unless the cows it comes from are free of abortion, they's goin' to be one hell of a big milk shortage."

The dry farmer family had finished their buying – two gallons of petrol and a lollipop apiece. They packed themselves into the sedan and rattled off to the west.

"Why don't you come over to our turkey shoot this Sunday?" asked Olsen of McLaughlin.

"Your wife gets all the prizes," kidded McLaughlin.

Olsen wagged his head proudly. "She's pretty good. But you have the name of bein' a fine shot yourself, Captain. You'd better try. There's always some officers from the Post comes out –"

Old Reuben Dale, their neighbour on the west, asked, "Any sign of mountain lions on your ranch this summer, McLaughlin? I've lost two calves out of the pasture on my place down near your Castle Rock Meadow, and I've got a notion it's a lion. Bert heerd a cat scream the other night when he went out to bring the cows in."

"Cats," said McLaughlin slowly. "No. I haven't seen any. Haven't heard any either, but I think I'm short of a colt –"

"They love horse meat," said Reuben, grinning.

As Ken and his father left the store with the mail and the yeast and tobacco and three lollipops and a peppermint patty for Nell, Ken looked up at his father. "What colt, Dad?"

McLaughlin didn't answer, and they got into the car. Ken asked again, "What colt are we short?"

"Rocket's. I think she had a foal. She hasn't got it now. Before I drive her out of the Stable Pasture, I'm going down to Castle Rock Meadow to take a look around."

Ken felt excited. He thought of the aspen grove, of Castle Rock, as big as an hotel, with all the caverns and passages and tunnels underneath it, and the skeletons and bones that lay in them. Wildcats –

McLaughlin was driving a little faster. Kennie glanced at him and saw that he had something of his hard angry look. His father was worried.

"What gun will you take, Dad?"

McLaughlin didn't answer for quite a long time, then said, "I'll take the Winchester. But I won't use it, Ken. The time you come on wildcat is the time you haven't got your gun with you."

Chapter Ten

Blow Flies rose, buzzing, as McLaughlin and the two boys stood looking down at all that was left of Rocket's foal. The hide was not yet dry; particles of flesh still clung to teeth and tiny hoofs; the hair of tail and mane lay in a swirl over the skeleton.

It was in one of the caves at the base of Castle Rock that Howard had come upon it, and after the first triumphant cry which called his father and Ken to him, they had stood without speaking, and there was no sound except for the angry humming of the flies that finally settled again on the carcass, shining, greenish, and busy.

"It was black," said Ken, stirring with his foot the little tail that was swirled over the bones.

Death, now. This might have been *his* colt. Gelding and death – what else?

"That's why Rocket wouldn't leave, isn't it, Dad?" said Howard.

"Guess so, son."

"Didn't she know it was dead?"

"She knew and she didn't know. Mares are funny about death. A mare won't hang around a dead foal or pay any attention to it. I've often thought they really don't recognize it or understand at all, but when they get far away from it, then they remember and begin to hunt and whinny for it."

McLaughlin squatted down and began to examine the carcass. The spinal cord was severed in two places at the base of the neck.

It had not been entirely eaten, the hide was intact on the haunches, the head crushed, parts of the bones of the legs scattered some distance around.

"Do you think it was a mountain lion killed it?" asked Ken.

"I think so. A wolf would have picked it cleaner. It didn't die of itself, that's sure, or it wouldn't have been in this cave. Something dragged it here. Plenty of game has been dragged in here to be eaten."

The place was a charnel house of bones, as were all the caverns under Castle Rock.

"Take a look around, boys, we'll see if we can figure out what killed it and how it happened. The ground here in the cave is too hard to show any prints."

Ken was glad to feel the air on his face as he emerged from the cave, and to get away from the smell, and the sound of the blow flies.

The day seemed to have changed and between the high

bank of light grey cloud and the earth was a scud of tattered dark clouds, racing from one mountain top to another.

"Going to rain," said McLaughlin.

Howard gave a shout. "Here's blood, Dad —" He pointed to a long red smear on a flat rock some distance from the cave.

McLaughlin grunted. "Dragged it across." The line from the rock and cave led down to the stream. On the strip of sandy beach where the stream had eaten under the bank they found four clear, round prints.

"There it is," said McLaughlin. "Mountain lion, really, though they call them wildcats around here. Look at the size of him."

The prints were big around as flapjacks.

Close by was the much trampled watering place of the horses, and here too, amongst the hoof prints, they found more of the prints of the lion.

Howard said excitedly, "Bet he killed it when the horses came here to water — jumped from the bank right on it —"

McLaughlin lit his pipe in his leisurely way, and then shook his head. "Wrong."

"Why?"

"Use your wits. A foal of that age — perhaps a week old — doesn't drink water."

"Well then, when Rocket came down to drink —"

"Rocket's a wildcat herself. If it had jumped her foal when she was close by she'd have attacked it. The cat would have been on the ground — she'd have cut it to pieces. What puzzles me is, where was Banner? If he'd seen the cat first, or smelled it, there'd have been a dead cat, not a dead colt. Banner must have been up at the other end of the meadow — Rocket off alone down here with the foal, and the cat was too quick for her — killed it —"

They reconstructed the scene. Rocket grazing. The colt separated from her, perhaps lying on the grass asleep — the sudden attack, the colt's scream — and Rocket rushing

86

to the rescue when it was too late – the cat's escape – the mare sniffing, hanging over the dead foal, then in bewilderment wandering away to hunt elsewhere.

"And then," said Howard, "when Rocket had gone away, the cat came back and dragged it away into the cave to eat it."

"And I guess that's the end of the mystery," said McLaughlin.

"But it's not the end of the mountain lion," said Ken. "Where is it, Dad?"

McLaughlin took out the little steel measuring tape he always carried, and measured the space between the prints of forefeet and hindfeet. "Five feet three," he said, putting the tape away. "A big fellow."

Both boys eyed their father, ready to take their cue from him. He seemed serious but not worried.

"That's what I'd like to know, Ken," he said, standing thoughtfully, puffing at his pipe, and looking all around, over at Dale's fence line, off at Castle Rock, and closer by through the aspen trees. "I'm glad I've got the brood mare bunch out of this meadow."

"Will the wildcat get others, Dad?"

"There's nothing here now for him to get. Everything's out on the range or up by the house. If the cat gets game enough here he'll stay here. Let's hope he will."

"What do they eat?"

"Everything that's alive. Even mice and gophers. They like a fresh kill, but they'll kill anything that moves, for fun if not for hunger."

"Can they get the horses and colts when they're on the range?"

"Not so easily where there's no cover. They hide and sneak up. Their only chance would be a surprise. If a horse saw them or smelled them first it could get away, because a cat's got no speed – legs too short. Now and then, if there's one horse off alone, a wildcat will attack it. They leap from the ground then, land on its neck, bite the spine through. A quick kill."

Suddenly there was an ear-splitting crash of thunder, and the rain poured down as if the explosion had burst a reservoir. The big round footprints of the wildcat melted and ran off in a slide of water.

As McLaughlin and the boys raced for the Studebaker, standing tilted on the hillside, Ken wondered if the cat was lurking somewhere near. He cast a glance backwards at Castle Rock. On those high battlements and ledges were no end of hiding places. The cat might be crouching there, watching all they did.

They got into the car and started off.

Castle Rock was a sinister and fascinating place. Ken and Howard had explored it from top to bottom many times, crawling through the underground passages, count-ing and studying the bones and skeletons in the caves, climbing up outside all over the high parapets and ledges, and still could not feel that they knew its secrets. On one of its ledges there trembled a huge boulder, as big as a locomotive, as smooth as a pebble. They had strained and heaved at it, convinced that a strong enough push would send it crashing off the ledge and caroming down.

One morning, soon after dawn, Ken, standing on top of the great rock, had seen five coyotes organize them-selves into a relay race and run down a rabbit in the mea-dow. They had stationed themselves at five points in a big circle, and had functioned in perfect team work, one coy-ote taking up the chase where the other dropped it, until the rabbit was exhausted, and had begun to bleat and squeal, making little futile dashes in this direction and that. Then the pack of coyotes had flung themselves on it like football players in a scrimmage; there was a moment's fierce nosing, biting, shoving; then the coyotes had come out of it and trotted off, and there were only a few bare white bones left on the meadow grass.

McLaughlin drove the Studebaker across the creek to

the southern side of the ranch and went back over the hills which led down to Deercreek and into the Stable Pasture, thinking to find Rocket and drive her out of the pasture without leaving the car.

Howard said, "The way she goes through fences or jumps them – even if we do get her out the pasture, she can come back in, can't she?"

"She can, and she does. That's the hell of having such a horse on the place."

"Then why do we do it?"

"It may hold her. Sometimes she minds the fences, sometimes she doesn't – just as she fancies – the thing is to get her up to the brood mares – Banner'll keep her there. He's the only one can manage her."

It was still raining hard, and as they cruised about through the woods, up and down the little trails through the Steppes, the boys could see that their father was losing his patience. The rain streamed down the windows of the car. Lightning split the skies and thunder came in peal after peal.

Rocket was nowhere in the Stable Pasture. They mounted their horses at last, Nell and Gus and Tim joined the hunt, and protected from the driving rain by oilskins they all scoured the woods and Steppes for an hour, but there was no sign of the mare, not even the usual clue she left behind her, a broken fence.

"For once, she's gone over the fence and not through it," said McLaughlin bitterly. "I'd like to know which way."

He sent Tim and Gus to do the milking and their evening chores, Nell and the boys to the house to get dry clothes on, and himself rode out on to the Saddle Back. If Rocket had joined the brood mare bunch of her own accord, there was nothing more to worry about; if not, she must be found.

The rain had stopped. The wind was sweeping all the clouds away and a perfect rainbow spanned the sky, framing the hill. Colour had come back to the ranch, the strong electric blue of the sky that in contrast made the roofs so red and the range so green and the pines so black.

McLaughlin, mounted on his big, nervous blood-bay mare, Taggert, galloped up the Saddle Back into the strange light that blazed down from the rainbow.

He had no idea where the mares were. They might be close at hand hidden in one of the depressions of the rolling land which were invisible to the eye at a little distance, or miles away. Suddenly he was amongst them. They were quiet, watching him. They had known someone was coming – one rider, Rob McLaughlin.

Banner was waiting for him and came forward immediately to meet him.

Taggert pricked her ears. Rob spoke to Banner, and sat quiet, looking about, counting the mares, searching for Rocket, while Banner and Taggert had a small interchange of civilities tinged with flirtatiousness, Banner asking impertinent questions, Taggert telling him to keep his distance.

A second rainbow shone out, almost as strongly coloured as the first, and the space between the two filled with a bright brown colour. There came the hint of a third rainbow.

Rocket was not there.

McLaughlin turned his mare and rode out of the bunch. Banner galloped behind him for a mile, then circled away and returned to his responsibilities.

When he had unsaddled, Rob gave orders to everyone to look for Rocket until she was found. The daily rides of Nell and the boys were to be directed to that end. Gus and Tim were to keep a look-out, wherever they happened to be working.

Rocket must be bred immediately, if possible on the ninth day after she had dropped her foal, so that she would foal early next season. A colt born late in the summer had

90

not the strength or growth enough to meet the early winter storms.

"And after that," said Rob. "I'll get that piece of rope off her neck."

He seemed to have lost his annoyance now that the day's work was done. He stamped about the kitchen, sniffing at the smell of fresh bread that filled it, but Nell, glancing at him, saw on his face the implacableness that she dreaded.

She got the bread knife and cut off the warm, crusty end of a loaf – smeared it thick with fresh sweet butter and handed it to him, smiling at the size of the bite that went into his mouth. But she was thinking of that bit of rope. What it was going to cost, measured in time and violence and fury, to get it off.

Lying beside Rob in the big walnut double bed that night, Nell had almost dropped off to sleep when she heard his voice.

"Nell –"

"Yes, dear?"

"This wildcat business – and the boys – what do you think?"

Her back was to him, but she could hear by his voice that he was wide awake and uneasy. He was up on one elbow.

"I know. I was thinking too. It scared me to death."

After a silence, "To tell them to be on the lookout – to get heavier guns for them – the twenty-twos would be no good – "

She finished for him. "It would just spoil the whole summer, wouldn't it?"

"They'd have to take their guns whenever they went out – "

"Yes."

"And even so – "

"That's it."

Silence again for a few moments. "There's probably hardly a chance of danger – only a chance in a hundred."

"Do they attack people, Rob?"

"Attack anything if they want to. They're incalculable. Cats, you know – "

"Can they really kill?"

"They can kill anything they can get the drop on – horse, cow, man – anything."

"But only when they're hungry, I suppose. And there's so much small game here – and the horses too – "

"Horseflesh is their favourite meat. Nell, I think I'll say nothing to them. I hate to put fear into them."

"They're mostly on horseback anyway, Rob."

"Yes."

Nell lay thinking it over. It did not seem to her an imminent danger. Just one more of the hazards of the mountain life. There was not a day that they were not in danger from something – Oh, God, watch over my boys – my three boys –

"Nell – "

Rob's voice was lower, and he moved closer, leaning over her. "There's *you* too – "

"Me?"

"You go out. Up in the Stable Pasture to read or walk – all afternoon alone – "

"Yes."

"And fishing. Hours off alone. In Deercreek, you walk along the stream there – trees overhead – "

"Yes – "

"Nell, I can't let you."

"Oh, Rob, I can't stay in – I have to go out – I have to feel free – "

"Not under the trees, Nell."

"They jump from trees, don't they?"

"Yes."

"Damn the thing – what a nuisance."

"Promise me, Nell – "

She reached a hand back and patted him. "I don't want you to be worried, dear — you have enough on your mind — but I'm really not a bit afraid."

"I know, but that's no help. Chances are, sooner or later, one of us will get a shot at it — if it comes up this end of the ranch. But meanwhile, don't go fishing in Deercreek. Fish in the meadows where the stream runs in the open and there are no trees."

"All right, dear."

"Promise?"

"I promise I won't fish in Deercreek." She laughed and closed her eyes again.

Always at night her fatigue was a positive pressing thing. She could feel it all through her, a heavy, sweet aching. And yielding to it was like sinking into a sucking depth.

Her thoughts began to scatter into grotesque formations like pieces of broken glass. She felt Rob's cheek on her hair. He was kissing her softly, all over her cheek and temple and down to the corner of her mouth.

He thinks I'm asleep, she thought, and breathed more evenly and deeply, her eyes closed. *So — dead — tired —* the deep place drawing her down into unconsciousness — Rob getting her all into his arms and the curve of his body — something moving in the thick foliage of the trees over Deercreek — a branch stirring gently — shadows — wind rushing through with a sound —

Chapter Eleven

The week that followed during which Ken was to choose his yearling was a busy one for everybody.

It rained every day out of one big purple cloud which drifted away at night, so that the mornings came in hot and clear, but by noon it was over the ranch again, and would start to rumble, then shiver and crack with lightning; then the downpour of rain, while the horizons all around were calm and blue, with fleecy white clouds motionless upon the hills.

Nell called it the Goose Bar sprinkling system. It brought out the strong, fresh colours of the flowers; dark salmon geraniums in the ultra-marine blue window boxes, and red, pink, purple and white petunias in the flower border. The roofs of the buildings were red and clean, with no dust on them, and the grass as green as a billiard table.

The boys were riding Lady and Calico and Buck and

Baldy, the horses that were being trained to rent for the Rodeo.

"When you're hunting for Rocket and looking over the yearlings and chasing the geldings you might well be training these plugs," said McLaughlin.

"Which shall we ride?" asked Howard.

McLaughlin, stretched out in a chair on the terrace with his pipe just before supper, gave this careful thought. "Now, let's see. Lady's nervous and she runs away. Went over backwards with Tim last week. Baldy, stubborn brute, argues with you but he's always right. More sense than a man. Calico, a running fool. Never knows when to stop. Wears himself out. Howard, you take Calico, and don't forget for a moment that he hasn't got sense. He'll be in a lather over nothing. Too willing. His mouth's hard. Don't encourage him to lean on the bit. Hold him in but don't carry his head. Talk to him a lot. He'll quiet down for the voice better than anything else. Ken, you take Lady. I'm giving her to you because most of the time you don't know where you are. You sit like a sack of meal, almost forget to hold the reins – she'll not know you're on her back. I've noticed when you're on her, she's never gathered. Goes about as if she was grazing. It's a good thing. Good for that mare, anyway. Eases her down. But watch out for her running away. Just don't let her get going too fast. When she does, it suddenly comes to her that she'll take the bit and run away; kind of goes to her head. I want to break her of that habit this summer. She's a fine horse."

"I'll help with Lady too," said Nell. "She always behaves well with me. I love to ride her. We understand each other."

"O.K. As a matter of fact, you could ride any of them, and it would be a good thing to change about. Any of you could ride Buck and Baldy. No use telling you what to do with Baldy, he'll do what he pleases, but it'll usually be the right thing. He won't object to orders unless

95

they're unreasonable. And Buck needs a lot of suppling and he's not as bridle-wise as he should be. Take them down into the practice field and do figure eights on them for an hour every other day. Just get them a bit quicker at answering the aids; more up and coming. Practice starts on the trot and the canter. Use saddles. Groom them before and after. Now remember, boys, this will be a daily duty for you, don't forget it, or neglect it, and I don't want to have to watch you or bother about it. You can keep the four of them in the Calf Pasture, they'll be handy to get at and won't get mixed with the other horses. Give them all the riding you can."

A Colorado buyer, Joe Williams, came to see if McLaughlin had any horses to sell. He came once or twice every year, collecting horses that he afterwards sold at the local auctions; but the prices he offered were so low that his appearance at the ranch was always the signal for Rob McLaughlin to lose his temper.

Williams offered thirty-five or forty dollars for an old brood mare with her spring colt; twenty or thirty for an old gelding broke for saddle and work provided his teeth were good enough to keep him in flesh; but as he paid cash down, and the only other way of getting anything at all for horses that were not fit for good markets was to ship them to the glue factory in a carload of old plugs and wild broncs dragged in off the range, McLaughlin, after hours of argument, loud words and insults, usually made a deal with him. Nell always urged him to. "After all," she said, "they're only getting older, and it's hard to keep them in condition, and he can get eight or ten of them into his truck, and even at his prices, that means a couple of hundred dollars."

On this occasion McLaughlin said that he'd get in some horses that were useless to him from his outlying pastures, and they'd make a deal; and Williams drove away, promising to be back inside of a week with his truck.

Jingo, the risling, died.

96

McLaughlin never allowed anyone to show, or even to feel, any grief about the death of the animals. It was an unwritten law to take death as the animals take it, all in the day's work, something natural and not too important; forget it. Close as they were to the animals, making such friends of them, if they let themselves mourn them, there would be too much mourning. Death was all around them – they did not shed tears.

But Jingo – the way he would come up behind you, nipping your shoulder, asking for attention – Ken could not forget him easily.

Gus tied a rope to the dead horse's head and fastened it to the back of the little Ford truck and hauled him away across the ranch to the shaft of the abandoned mine on the hillside, three hundred feet deep –

The really big event of the week was that McLaughlin engaged a bronco-buster to break the three-year-olds.

Ken saw the man first when they were coming down from the stables just before supper one evening, and the bronco-buster was standing on the Green talking to Nell.

He was very small and neat. His legs were thin and bowed in tight blue jeans that were rubbed to light blue inside the thighs and on the seat. His waist was not much larger than Ken's and was belted snug. His small face was bright red and blank-looking. His blue eyes were so direct they made other eyes seem shifty.

Nell introduced him, just saying that this was Ross Buckley who was going to ride in the Rodeo and had a couple of weeks of free time right now, waiting for the Rodeo, and thought he would put it in breaking some horses.

"I heerd you-all had some hot-bloods up here," said Ross in a pleasant drawling voice. "Thought I'd like to have a try at 'em, if you've got any that need breaking."

Nell said, "Come on, Howard and Ken – time to clean up for supper," and walked away with the boys, leaving McLaughlin there talking to Ross.

Ross had arrived in a Ford sedan piled to the roof with

97

saddles and bridles and blankets and lariats, and when Nell had talked to him and found out what he wanted, she kept him there until McLaughlin came down from the stables.

McLaughlin engaged him, and took him up to the bunk house and introduced him to Gus and Tim, and every day since he had been working in the corral at the broncs.

And in addition to all this, hours had been spent every day, looking for Rocket; but no one had seen hide nor hair of her.

Ken had not yet been able to decide on his colt.

Rocket had her filly hidden away with her in a little valley near the Colorado border.

There was deep meadow grass in the bottom, timothy and red-top; there was gamma grass on the sides of the slopes that shut them in; there was, best of all, high clover at the base of the hill above where a spring burst through the ground in a dozen bubbling holes.

The water loitered in winding runlets, and at last joined to make a little stream, and the stream made a bed of moist earth for a copse of cottonwoods and aspen, and the shade and moisture made food and cover for a thicket of raspberry and gooseberry bushes and wildflowers; bluebells with yard-long stems as fine as hairs, white Mariposa lilies with pansy dark hearts, and the wild forget-me-not blossome like tiny seeds of turquoise, and larkspur - pink, white, and blue – death to cattle and horses.

The filly nosed the larkspur, breathing in its scent, then blew out her breath, snorting, and moved over to the clover and feasted. She stood shoulder deep, green stems and yellow blossoms sticking out on either side of her mouth as she chewed, her head up, looking around contentedly.

She had only nursed a few times. Rocket was not so imperative now that the first agony was relieved and the milk drying up. The two horses – big black mare and little orange one, grazed side by side in the meadow, and drank at the springs, and cantered on the hill-sides, standing now and again on the crests with eyes alert and ears sharply pointed.

They were not alone in the valley. In the copse twittered wild canaries and bluebirds. Half a dozen handsome black and white magpies argued noisily in the cottonwoods; a flock of goldfinch swooped across the valley, warbling; swung upwards, circled around, and disappeared over one of the hills, only to appear from a different direction and make the round again. Small game moved in the grass; in the sky were a pair of hawks on the watch; and two antelope were feeding in the valley, curious and dainty as porcelain figurines.

On the day that her foal would have been nine days old, Rocket cantered up one of the hills and stood at the top, looking over.

When the filly came up beside her, the mare bared her teeth and nipped at her. The filly moved away, and Rocket continued her searching of the wind and the plains.

The filly lay down and went to sleep.

Rocket made the round of the hilltops, at a gallop. On one crest she stood and neighed loudly.

It was the northerly outlook that held her eyes the longest. The ranch lay due north. *Banner* was north. . . . Before evening she and the filly had left their valley and were working north, pausing to graze and water, not hurrying.

Chapter Twelve

Ken wakened one morning in the dark and turned to face the window, and when it showed faintly grey outside, he got up and stood watching the dawn brighten in the east.

Ken never dreamed at night. He often wondered why, and asked his mother. "Howard dreams, and you and Dad; and I heard Tim telling about a crazy dream he had – why don't I ever dream?"

His mother had looked at him oddly and said, "When you dream, it's dreams of another sort – at a different time."

"Why?"

But she didn't seem to know why any more than he did.

He stood with his face at the screen, shivering a little and feeling excited, because he was going to go out. He could see that the weather had changed.

There were small, tattered, low-flying black clouds, as

if the one big cloud had been torn to pieces; there were a few stars going in and out between them; and behind all the clouds a greenish glow spread upwards from the horizon.

There wasn't enough light yet for him to see anything clearly. It seemed a world of near-darkness, in which vague outlines appeared and vanished, floating and shadowy. His thoughts were like that, too. He groped for familiar footing in his mind, but everything was changed. Something new had come into him so that he was different. Even Tim said that he had grown an inch since his father promised him the colt, and Howard treated him as if he was important. But something had gone out of him, too; and sometimes he wanted it so that he was in a panic.

It was a place he used to play and be happy in; quite secret, no one knew he was there; and safe, because he had everything his own way; pleasant, because there were no unhappy endings. In the real world just about everything had an unhappy ending or tripped him up somehow, but *there*, there were no endings at all – dreams don't end – one piles on another – dreams just drift, like a picture or a view with mist over it, and then, in the mist, another picture taking shape – always one putting the other out – never an end.

He had been, in a way, trying to get back to this place all week, as if it was his last chance –

But now he was outside. The door was shut. It was windy and dangerous outside – The colt – he began to dress hurriedly. Today or tomorrow he must choose his colt. He would ride up now on to the range and look at the yearlings again.

It was still dark when he stole out the front door and felt the terrace grass under his feet. No one had heard him. That was good. He didn't want Howard along. Going out in the early morning was almost like going into the underwater world, or the world of a picture, or in a dream. Not quite so safe as a dream because he did have to watch his horse, or, if he was climbing on Castle Rock, he had to be careful of his footing, but still nothing like the ordinary world of the daytime.

He walked softly across the Green to the Calf Pasture to get his horse.

Ken had been a night wanderer ever since he had learned to walk alone and to climb over the edge of his crib. Nell would wake, hearing a sound in the hall or living-room, would find the baby's crib empty and go searching for him.

She'd find him somewhere in the dark, crawling or stand-ing unsteadily on the tail of his nightgown and would pick him up and carry him back to bed.

She tried tying the bottom of his nightgown in a knot with his feet inside, but he merely became more expert at balancing. Then she hobbled him with a soft diaper, but he learned to swing both feet together over the side of his crib, hang with little monkey hands, drop down, and shuffle instead of walk.

When he was older, sometimes he'd go outdoors in the night.

Often Nell did that herself. Restless or unable to sleep, she would slip from her bed, tie a robe around her, take pillow and blanket and go down to her hammock, and lie with her face to the sky, watching the stars.

Ken found Lady just inside the fence of the Calf Pas-ture, and when he held out his hand and spoke to her, she didn't move away but let him take hold of her halter and lead her out.

He had been riding Lady all week when he was exercis-ing the geldings and looking for Rocket and inspecting the yearlings. He had gone to look at the yearlings every day, and yesterday his mother had ridden out with him. They hadn't been able to find them anywhere, until suddenly, from a high place, they heard the thunder of hoofs.

"They sounded like a regiment," said Nell, telling about it at supper. "And we looked down and saw them, a stream of colour flying down the draw. It was beautiful to watch them! They shone in the sun – sorrel and black and bay and roan – the flowing movement – so gay, so free, so frolic-some!"

And then they had ridden down to the yearlings and dis-mounted among them, and Nell exclaimed upon the way their first year of life changed their appearance – dark chestnuts turned to sorrels, a pink roan changed to a blue, blacks lightened to brown, odd spots and marking vanished completely; and conformation altered almost beyond re-cognition.

"They look stunning," she told Rob. "Smooth and sleek and glossy, their little hides so full and taut they look as if they would burst."

Ken himself had been dazed by the beauty of them. The rich feeling – one of them his own, but which? He wanted them all, and until he chose, in a way, they were all his.

Ken led Lady up the little path through the Gorge, into the corrals, and then into the dark stable, put the catch on her halter, poured a measure of oats in the feed box in the manger before her, and began to groom her. Dad said use saddles – can't see why – better do it anyway –

Lady was a big red roan with a black tail and mane. She moved quickly, her head had a proud, high carriage; her dark eyes were full and intelligent.

Ken slid around her, close to her haunches, one hand on her tail, and then gave her a whack and said, "Get over!"

The mare moved over with her quick strong step and Ken rubbed down her other side. He put on the saddle blan-ket, then the saddle, and cinched it as tight as he could, remembering the blanket he had lost; lastly the bridle – she had finished her oats. He led her out of the corral and shut the gate. There was a rock there upon which he often stood to mount the tallest horses. He led Lady up to it. First he tried the cinch again. Loose! She always blew herself up when she was being saddled. That was what he had

103

forgotten to do the other day with Cigarette. He took the cinch up three more holes, mounted, and moved off.

The four broncs that Ross was breaking were grazing in the Stable Pasture close by the corrals, and when they saw him, they trotted over to him, and Ken drew rein and stood there, letting them come up and sniff and nicker at Lady; and she nickered back. When he went on they followed for a little while, and then turned back to the corrals – waiting for their oats, he thought. Ross always gave each one a measure of oats before he worked them. Their names were Gangway, Don, Rumba and Blazes.

Sometimes, Ken thought, as he cantered towards the County Road gate, the names his mother gave the colts in their first summer didn't stick, because the colts changed so. There had been Irish Elegance, so smooth and classy-looking the first summer that Nell said she was naming him after a beautiful, copper-coloured, California rose. But the second summer he had turned into a little mick, so they dropped the *Elegance* and just call him *Irish*.

Ross was having a tough time breaking Gangway, a big blood bay out of Taggert, the tallest and handsomest of the four. Yesterday Ken and Howard had sat on the corral fence watching Ross working with him. Gangway was bucking, and Ross had called to Howard to open the corral gate and let him out. The horse bucked out the gate with him, and Ross swung his quirt, and spurred him, and Gangway sun-fished and cork-screwed and jack-knifed. Ross sat with a little grin and his quirt going all the time, and when he came past Ken, exploding in great grass-hopper leaps, he said, "Might's well keep him goin' and git it outen his system."

When it was over and he had ridden Gangway back into the corral and dismounted, Ross went over to the fence and stood hanging on to it, vomiting.

Ken had to dismount to open the gate to the County Road. He was careful to hold the rein tight as he led Lady through and closed the gate behind him. He found another rock to mount by and started up the Saddle Back.

All the clouds had turned pink, and behind them the sky was a faraway, fiery blue.

The higher he climbed the wider the sky was, and the farther stretched the fleet of tattered clouds. They were getting more colour every minute, some of them blazed crimson. All the stars had disappeared except one, which shone between two clouds, bright gold.

Lady wanted her head.

There was a strong current of sympathy between the boy and the mare. When he wanted to stop and look around she understood perfectly and stood with ears pricked and head turning, absorbed in contemplation just as he was. And at exactly the moment when he had had enough, she knew it, and would move forward without the signal.

Today she was excited by the colour and the electric quality of the air and the feeling of movement in the grass and the sky, and she kept asking for a free rein. When Ken gave it to her, she stretched out her nose and went up the steepest part of the Saddle Back at a gallop.

Ken looked for the yearlings where they had been yesterday but there was no sign of them. He rode around for an hour, thinking that Shorty would have taken him right to them, but Lady didn't have that much sense, she was just excited and wanting to run in any direction. All the sunrise colours had gone now, and the torn shreds of clouds were purple and grey and stormy looking.

Ken rode up to the highest peak of the Saddle Back so that he could look all around for dozens of miles; but the range was empty; not a head of stock anywhere. Still, he knew they could be hidden in the folds of the hills and never show an ear – but which fold? Which hill?

He rode on, and suddenly, coming around a curve, he saw Banner standing out in front of the brood mares, intent and alert, gathered for action.

Ken had barely time to turn his head when he saw Rocket

and a sorrel filly cantering towards the bunch, and then he saw Banner trot out to meet them with lowered head and an expression of irresistible intention in his whole body.

Rocket and the young sorrel halted together. Rocket whinnied. Banner screamed. His head snaked along the grass. He reached them and circled around them both. Rocket began to gallop away. Banner pursued, first on one side of her then on the other. The sorrel colt clung to its mother's side, whinnying nervously. She got in Banner's way. He gave a vicious, snarling neigh, plunged at the little one and bit it in the ribs. It screamed and fled, Banner pursuing.

Lady was taut and trembling with excitement, as Ken was himself. The brood mares, too, were motionless, watching the chase.

The filly showed Banner a clean pair of heels. How she could run!

Rocket trotted nervously up and down near the brood mares. The filly made a big circle, with Banner thundering after her. She came back to the mares, and as she passed them Banner swerved and went for Rocket. The filly fled past Ken. He saw frightened eyes in a tangle of streaming hair and slim legs, and a pang went through him. For a fraction of a second she had looked at him, and it was like an appeal. He wheeled his mount and followed her, turning in the saddle to look back at Rocket.

Rocket was cantering away again with Banner close beside her and before the curve of a hill shut them from view, Ken saw her come to a stop, and the great body of the stallion rear over her. For a moment the two of them, twisted into one shape, were sculptured against the stormy sky.

When Ken turned and looked again for the filly she was nowhere in sight. He pulled Lady up short. The range was empty, with no movement but the clouds and the grass, and no sound but the panting of the mare he rode and the thud of his own heart beating.

Rocket's colt – a yearling, a filly – and *his own*. He hadn't had to choose one after all. She had just come to him. His own because of that second's cry for help that had come from her eyes to his; his own because of her wild beauty and speed, his own because his heart burned with him at the sight and thought of her; his own because – well, just his own.

Then, from far ahead of him came an excited whinny – another and another. The filly appeared from nowhere, a tiny shape, running on a ridge in front of him, tail streaming against the dark tattered clouds; she plunged over the ridge, he heard more whinnies, he kicked Lady in the ribs and gave her her head, and in a few moments stood on the ridge, looking down, and saw the beautiful filly rejoining the band of yearlings, who welcomed her with excited chatterings as school-children welcome each other at reunion in the fall.

Ken rode down the mountain in a daze of happiness. No dream he had ever had, no imagination of adventure or triumph could touch this moment. He felt as if he had burst out of his old self and was something entirely new – and that the world had burst into something new too. So this was it – this was what being alive meant – Oh, my filly, my filly, my beautiful –

Chapter Thirteen

"For once you're back to breakfast on time," said Rob, as Ken took his seat at the table.

Nell filled Ken's bowl with oatmeal and passed it to him.

Ever since she had read in the Government bulletins that all prize stock was raised on elaborate formulas of mixed grains – *or ground oats* – and had noticed that the dogs, when they were hungry, squirmed through the wire fence into the calves' corral and ate the ground oats from the feed boxes, oatmeal had a place on her breakfast table. If you can raise good calves and colts on it, I guess you can raise boys, she reasoned. And McLaughlin, with a long line of oat-eating Scottish ancestors behind his brawn and toughness, agreed.

With the oatmeal there was always a big pitcher of yellow Guernsey cream and a bowl of brown sugar. Nell, smiling, pushed them towards Ken, noticing the unusual colour in his face. the boy flashed a glance at his mother; his eyes were dark with excitement. His whole face was lit up – transfigured really – and she felt a slight sense of shock. What had happened? He had been different all week, more sure of himself, more alert and happy, but this –

Rob McLaughlin was looking at Ken too, not missing a thing. Something had happened that morning on the range –

"What horse did you ride?" he asked.

"Lady."

"And where is she now? On her way to the border?" jocularly.

"I put her in the Home Pasture. She's out there at the fountain now."

"Was she hot?"

"No, sir, I cooled her off coming home." There was a little smile of pride on Ken's face, and Nell thought, all the right answers, so far.

The examination went on. "Did you give her a good workout?"

"Yes, sir."

"Then don't ride her again today. Take Baldy if you want a horse."

"Yes, sir."

"Break anything? Lose anything?"

"No, sir."

Rob laughed. He leaned over and patted Ken on the head. "Good work, young man – coming along! "

Ken burst out laughing. He was so excited it was hard to sit still and answer properly. He wasn't going to tell about his colt yet – not till tomorrow when the week was up. But it was hard to hold it in, hard not to jump up and run around the kitchen, shouting and crowing. Anyway – he could tell about Rocket –

"I didn't *lose* anything, I *found* something! " He boasted, shovelling in big spoonfuls of oatmeal. "I found Rocket. She's back."

"Where?" demanded Rob and Nell and Howard all together.

"With the brood mares."

"Good," said McLaughlin. "Let's see – what day would this be after her colt, Nell?"

"If the colt was less than a week old when she lost it," calculated Nell.

"Yes – and then this past week – yes, somewhere between the ninth and fourteenth day. That's about it," McLaughlin grinned. "So the wild woman came back of herself."

"She came up from the South, and Banner went out to get her. She's bred already."

"I'll say she is," said McLaughlin.

Nell went to the stove, lifted the bacon out of the hot fat and laid it on a platter. "Orders, please," she cried.

"*Two on a raft and wreck 'em!*" shouted Rob jovially, with his big, white-toothed smile.

"*One, looking at you!*" shouted Ken hilariously.

Howard jumped up. "I'll do yours *over and easy*, Mother –" No one could do Nell's egg to suit her like Howard. She liked it lightly fried on one side, then lightly on the other, not broken. It had to be flipped. Rob could flip them but he made a big to-do about it and tossed them high and many a one landed on the stove or the edge of the skillet. Howard poured a little of the hot bacon grease into a one-egg skillet and broke an egg in. While it crackled and spat, he salted it carefully, and in a moment loosened the curling brown edges, then with a smooth motion of his wrist, gave the pan a lift and a thrust, and the egg rose a few inches into the air, turned a slow somersault, and slid back into the fat.

Carrying the hot plates with holders, Nell distributed the eggs, and set the bacon on the table. She was still thinking about Ken, and kept looking at him. Every time he caught her eye, he smiled blissfully. He was all excited – there was something he was not telling – something he had

110

seen out on the range that morning – the colt, of course, the colt –

"Nell," said Rob, "are you very busy this morning?"

"Nothing special – no baking or cleaning – why?"

"How'd you like to break a bronc for me?"

Nell looked up quickly. "One of the four? That little mare, Rumba?"

"Yes."

"I'd love to!"

"Why doesn't Ross do it?" asked Howard.

"Ross is too tough." Rob's face looked grim. "I'm not going to let him monkey with her. I've stood all I can with the other three – I wouldn't be surprised if Don's knees are damaged."

"Not permanently?" cried Nell.

"Well, it'll take a long time for the swelling to go down. He threw himself about so. And, all tied up the way Ross had him he kept falling on his knees. I had to walk away – couldn't look at it. Don't like to interfere with a man when he's been hired to do a job and is doing it his own way, but I couldn't stick it. The little mare – why her feet would fit in a tea cup, as dainty as a fawn. And her forelegs –" he picked up Ken's arm, "about as big round as Ken's wrist."

"She's a very funny, special little mare," said Nell. "I remember her last summer when you brought her in to halter-break her. She fell in the water trough on her back and wouldn't get up."

Ken remembered too, laughing, "Yes – she stayed there all afternoon with her feet sticking straight up."

Howard persisted, "Then why don't you do it, Dad?"

"I'm far too heavy, Howard. I've been on her and taught her a bit, and she's used to the saddle all right but she needs a light rider; and she's afraid of Ross – even if I didn't let him tie her up. She shakes every time she sees him."

"Could I ride her?" asked Howard.

"You're light enough, but it isn't only the actual weight.

111

There's something a bit heavy handed about you, Howard. I saw you give Calico's head a bad jerk the other day."

Howard scowled. "He was swinging his head up and down. I hate that."

"So you punished him?"

Howard nodded. McLaughlin said quietly, "Sometimes one has to punish a horse. Calico's got a bad habit with his head, but you gave him more than he needed. Little Rumba couldn't take anything like that at this stage of her training. It might start her bucking, and I don't want her ever to buck. She needs to be reassured and just held nicely, and sort of coaxed."

"What about me?" demanded Ken.

McLaughlin laughed. "Why you'd go off into a dream and the horse could run away with you and you wouldn't know it until ten miles later you'd wake up and wonder where you were. What you've got, Ken, is fine hands, but no control. Rumba needs someone with authority. Your mother's got that, and hands like yours, and she's lighter in the saddle than any of you – not pounds, but balance; seat. I want you both in the corral when your mother rides Rumba. You'll learn something."

When Nell walked up to the stables she was dressed in well-cut jodhpurs made of carefully softened and faded blue-jean denim. Suitable clothes for her ranch life had been hard to find. She hated to be untidy – hated to be constrained; boots and breeches she found too heavy and binding, so she had her white linen jodhpurs (from Abercrombie and Fitch) copied by a local tailor in blue-jean material. She had half a dozen pairs of these; they were nearly indestructible, light enough to be cool, washed perfectly, and were very becoming to her slender, free-moving body. A darker blue jersey polo shirt with very short sleeves left her brown arms bare; she wore pigskin gloves, a round blue linen hat with a narrow brim to pull down over her eyes and stick on against the Wyoming winds – (it was said by the local wits that, in Wyoming, you can tell a stranger from a native because the stranger, if his hat blows off, will pursue it) – and on her feet, under the straps of her trousers, soft tan jodhpur shoes with small chainless spurs set into the leather of the heel. Even so, long before the day was done she was weary of the denim and leather, and was glad to get back into light cotton dresses.

Rumba, saddled and bridled, was waiting, tied to the post. Ross came riding into the corral on Gangway, and dismounted.

"Mornin', Missus," he said to Nell, managing to convey both gallantry and deference in his slow drawling voice; and Nell again thought, with a little glow of pleasure, that *Missus* was a royal title in the West. Ross, by the very tilt of his small body as he faced her, put himself at her service.

"How's the pony this morning?" asked McLaughlin.

"A bit spooky and a little stiff – but travellin' all right."

"Mother's going to ride Rumba," said Ken.

Ross's eyes moved quickly to Rumba, then to McLaughlin. He busied himself loosening the cinch on Gangway, and said quietly, "She ain't ready to ride yet. She ain't been sacked out with her feet tied, like I done with Gangway and the others."

McLaughlin said quietly, "Rumba's feet are too small and her legs too delicate to tie up."

"I wouldn't ride her myself," insisted Ross, "lessen I was in a Rodeo and paid to. Them hot-bloods is worse than broncs if once they git to buckin'."

"I think she'll be all right," said McLaughlin. "Mrs. McLaughlin's about the right weight; she's a little timid, but she won't have any trouble."

"Timid!" marvelled Ross. "I put my wife on a ole plug once that was broke pretty fair, and it got to runnin' a little, and she busted out cryin' and came back bawlin'. Did I get it!"

"You don't look old enough to have a wife, Ross," said Nell.

"I got a wife and two kids 'bout half as big as Howard and Ken," said Ross grinning. "I'm twenty-five. My brother's twenty-six."

Ross rolled himself a cigarette and sat down against the corral fence. Howard and Ken climbed up and sat on the top railing. Nell walked over to Rumba, and Rob stood beside Ross talking to him, and pretending not to watch.

Rumba became taut, her ears forward, looking at Nell, her head up as if she was on the point of rearing, and her hind legs crouching. Nell held out a hand and talked to her reassuringly, but when the hand touched her head, Rumba jerked up. Nell kept stroking her and talking to her until at last the mare was quiet and her trembling and crouching stopped. Nell turned her back to her, leaning against the post, and stood there talking to Rob and Ross, to give the mare a chance to get used to her body and her voice. Under the eye of a human being an unbroken horse is in terror.

"Is your brother a bronco-buster too, Ross?"

"No, Ma'am, he ain't got the heart. You just gotta have the heart fur it."

"Do you do a lot of it, Ross?"

"Sure do, Ma'am – all summer long. All over the country, wherever there's a show. One summer I made a thousand dollars. As soon as one Rodeo's over, I'm itchin' to git to the next. Everyone says I'll git killed, but, hell, what's the difference? Better than work at that –"

Rumba, feeling more free now because no eye was upon her, reached out her nose and Nell felt the soft muzzle against her back between the shoulders. She paid no attention, but Rumba, as if alarmed by the smell of her, jumped back.

Ross was talking about the Rodeo Riders' Union, called COWBOYS' TURTLE ASSOCIATION, to which he belonged. At a Texas Rodeo, they struck for a share of the gate receipts in addition to the prize money. This held up the show for a couple of hours, but they won out.

Rumba tried again. This time she was bolder and took a

long breath, drawing in the very essence of the human being who, she knew in advance, was going to mount her.
Nell knew that if a horse hates the smell of a person it is
hardly possible to make friends. On the other hand, if he
likes it, friendship is only a matter of time and patience.

Obviously Nell passed the test, for Rumba rested then,
with her nose touching Nell's arm, her eyes and ears directed to the men who were talking, indulging her natural
curiosity. Rob did not want the little mare to feel she
was the centre of attention. He said horses were like
people – no one liked to feel all eyes upon them except
show-offs, like Gangway, who always expected to be
watched.

"Don't you ever get hurt, bronco bustin'?" asked
Howard, his feet dangling over Ross's head from where
he sat on the fence rail above him.

"I'll say," was the laconic answer. "Last summer I hurt
myself in every show I was in –"

"Break anything?"

"Ribs, collar bone – back hurt – knee wrenched. Spent
most of my time in hospital. When I went in fur the third
trip last summer, I was broke. They waan't goin' to let
me out till I'd paid my bill. I says, You might as well let
me out for I ain't got no way to make money layin' here in
hospital, I got to git ridin' before I kin pay you off. Well,
they wouldn't. An' they was arguin' with me, and I says,
You call up the Rodeo Committee here, and tell 'em about
me not bein' able to pay my bill. Well, I guess they did, for
they let me out, and I never heard nuthin' more about the
bill, neither."

Nell turned around to Rumba and saw that the mare had
accepted her. She no longer shivered, but kept her eyes on
Nell without fear. Nell gathered up the reins, still stroking
her and talking to her. She went to the side, put both arms
on top of the saddle and leaned there, now and then lifting
her knee up under the mare's belly as if she was going to
mount.

115

Rumba showed no alarm. Her head was turned a little, one eye back watching Nell.

Now Rob joined her and held Rumba's head. Nell put her foot in the stirrup, mounted very slowly, swung her leg over the haunch, got her seat, and Rob untied the halter rope from the post and adjusted the stirrups.

A little pressure of the legs, a little urging with voice and hands, and Rumba started off slowly. Nell was careful to hold the reins fairly short so that, in case the mare took a sudden notion to buck, she could not get her head down. They made the round of the corral several times, then Rob opened the gate, he and Ross mounted Don and Gangway, and all three rode down to the practice field for a morning's work.

Chapter Fourteen

When Ken went to bed that night, he kissed his mother, and then threw his arms around her and held her fiercely for a moment.

Smiling, she put her hand on his head. "Well, Kennie –" her violet eyes were soft and understanding.

He went upstairs, smiling back at her over his shoulder, having a secret with her. He knew that she knew.

He lit the candle in his room and stood staring at the flickering light. This was like a last day. The last day before school is out, or before Christmas, or before his mother came back after a visit in the East. Tomorrow was the day when, really, his life would begin. He would get his colt.

He had been thinking about the filly all day. He could still see her streaking past him, the wild terrified eyes turned to him in appeal – the hair blown back from her

117

face like a girl's – and the long, slim legs moving so fast they were a blur, like the spokes of a wheel.

He couldn't quite remember the colour of her. Orange – pink – tangerine colour – tail and mane white, like the hair of an Albino boy at school. *Albino* – of course, her grandsire *was* the Albino – the famous Albino stud. He felt a little uneasiness at this; Albino blood wasn't safe blood for a filly to have. But perhaps she hadn't much of it. Perhaps the cream tail and mane came from Banner, her sire. Banner had a cream tail and mane too when he was a colt; lots of sorrel colts had. He hoped she would be docile and good – not like Rocket. Which would she take after? Rocket? Or Banner? He hadn't had time to get a good look into her eyes. Rocket's eyes had that wild, wicked, white ring around them –

Ken began to undress. Walking around his room, his eyes caught sight of the pictures on the wall – they didn't interest him.

The speed of her! *She had run away from Banner*. He kept thinking about that. It hardly seemed possible. His father always said Rocket was the fastest horse on the ranch, and now Rocket's filly had run away from Banner.

He had gone up to look at her again that afternoon, hadn't been able to keep away. He had ridden up on Baldy and found the yearlings all grazing together on the far side of Saddle Back. An when they saw him and Baldy, they all took off across the mountain.

Ken had galloped along the crest above them watching the filly. Footing made no difference to her. She floated across the ravines, always two lengths ahead of the others. Her pinkish cream mane and tail whipped in the wind. Her long delicate legs had only to aim, it seemed, at a particular spot, for her to reach it and sail on. She seemed to Ken a fairy horse. She was simply nothing like any of the others.

Riding down the mountain again Ken had traced back all his recollections of her. The summer before, when he and Howard had seen the spring colts, he hadn't especially noticed her. He remembered that he had seen her even before that, soon after she was born. He had been out with Gus, one day, in the meadow, during the spring holiday. They were clearing some driftwood out of the irrigation ditch, and they had seen Rocket standing in a gully on the hillside, quiet for once, and eyeing them cautiously.

"Ay bet she got a colt," said Gus; and they walked carefully up the draw. Rocket gave a wild snort, thrust her feet out, shook her head wickedly, then fled away. And as they reached the spot, they saw standing there the wavering, pinkish colt, barely able to keep its feet. It gave a little squeak and started after its mother on crooked, wobbling legs.

"Yeewhiz! Look at de little *flicka!*" said Gus.

"What does *flicka* mean, Gus?"

"Swedish for little gurl, Ken –"

He had seen the filly again late in the fall. She was half pink, half yellow – with streaked untidy looking hair. She was awkward and ungainly, with legs too long, haunches a little too high.

And then he had gone away to school and hadn't seen her again until now – *she ran away from Banner* Her eyes – they had looked like balls of fire this morning. What colour were they? Banner's were brown with flecks of gold, or gold with flecks of brown – Her speed and her delicate curving lines made him think of a greyhound he had seen running once, but really she was more like just a little girl than anything – the way her face looked, the way her blonde hair blew – a little girl –

Ken blew out the light and got into bed, and before the smile had faded from his face, he was asleep –

"I'll take that sorrel filly of Rocket's; the one with the cream tail and mane."

Ken made his announcement at the breakfast table.

After he spoke there was a moment's astonished silence. Nell groped for recollection, and said, "A sorrel filly? I

119

can't seem to remember that one at all – what's her name?"

But Rob remembered. The smile faded from his face as he looked at Ken. "*Rocket's filly*, Ken?"

"Yes, sir." Ken's face changed too. There was no mistaking his father's displeasure.

"I was hoping you'd make a wise choice. You know what I think of Rocket – that whole line of horses –"

Ken looked down; the colour ebbed from his cheeks. "She's fast, Dad, and Rocket's fast –"

"It's the worst line of horses I've got. There's never one amongst them with real sense. The mares are hellions and the stallions outlaws; they're untamable."

"I'll tame her."

Rob guffawed. "Not I, nor anyone, has ever been able to really tame any one of them."

Kennie's chest heaved.

"Better change your mind, Ken. You want a horse that'll be a real friend to you, don't you?"

"Yes –" Kennie's voice was unsteady.

"Well, you'll never make a friend of that filly. Last fall after all the colts had been weaned and separated from their dams, she and Rocket got back together – no fence'll hold 'em – she's all out and scarred up already from tearing through barbed wire after that bitch of a mother of hers."

Kennie looked stubbornly at his plate.

"Change your mind?" asked Howard briskly.

"No."

"I don't remember seeing her this year," said Nell.

"No," said Rob. "When I drove you up a couple of months ago to look them over and name them and write down their descriptions, there was a bunch missing, don't you remember?"

"Oh, yes – then she's never been named –"

"I've named her," said Ken. "Her name is Flicka."

"Flicka," said Nell cheerfully. "That's a pretty name."

120

But McLaughlin made no comment, and there was a painful silence.

Ken felt he ought to look at his father, but he was afraid to. Everything was changed again, they weren't friends any more. He forced himself to look up, met his father's angry eyes for a moment, then quickly looked down again.

"Well," McLaughlin barked. "It's your funeral – or hers. Remember one thing. I'm not going to be out of pocket on account of this – every time you turn around you cost me money –"

Ken looked up, wonderingly, and shook his head.

"Time's money, remember," said his father. "I had planned to give you a reasonable amount of help in breaking and taming your colt. Just enough. But there's no such thing as enough with those horses."

Gus appeared at the door and said, "What's today, Boss?"

McLaughlin shouted, "We're going out on the range to bring in the yearlings. Saddle Taggert, Lady and Shorty."

Gus disappeared, and McLaughlin pushed his chair back. "First thing to do is get her in. Do you know where the yearlings are?"

"They were on the far side of the Saddle Back late yesterday afternoon – the west end, down by Dale's ranch."

"Well, you're the Boss on this round-up – you can ride Shorty."

McLaughlin and Gus and Ken went out to bring the yearlings in. Howard stood at the County gate to open and close it.

They found the yearlings easily. When they saw that they were being pursued, they took to their heels. Ken was entranced to watch Flicka – the speed of her, the power, the wildness – she led the band.

He sat motionless, just watching and holding Shorty in when his father thundered past on Taggert and shouted,

121

"Well, what's the matter? Why didn't you turn 'em?"

Ken woke up and galloped after them.

Shorty brought in the whole band. The corral gates were closed, and an hour was spent shunting the ponies in and out and through the chutes until Flicka was left alone in the small round branding corral. Gus mounted Shorty and drove the others away, through the gate, and up the Saddle Back.

But Flicka did not intend to be left. She hurled herself against the poles which walled the corral. She tried to jump them. They were seven feet high. She caught her front feet over the top rung, clung, scrambled, while Kennie held his breath for fear the slender legs would be caught between the bars and snapped. Her hold broke, she fell over backwards, rolled, screamed, tore around the corral.

One of the bars broke. She hurled herself again. Another went. She saw the opening, and as neatly as a dog crawls through a fence, inserted her head and forefeet, scrambled through and fled away, bleeding in a dozen places.

As Gus was coming back, just about to close the gate to the County Road, the sorrel whipped through it, sailed across the road and ditch with her inimitable floating leap, and went up the side of the Saddle Back like a jack rabbit.

From way up the mountain, Gus heard excited whinnies, as she joined the band he had just driven up, and the last he saw of them they were strung out along the crest running like deer.

"Yee whiz!" said Gus, and stood motionless and staring until the ponies had disappeared over the ridge.

Then he closed the gate, remounted Shorty, and rode back to the corrals.

Walking down from the corrals, Rob McLaughlin gave Kennie one more chance to change his mind. "Better pick a horse that you have some hope of riding one day. I'd have got rid of this whole line of stock if they weren't so damned fast that I've had the fool idea that someday there might turn out one gentle one in the lot, and I'd have a race horse. But there's never been one so far, and it's not going to be Flicka."

"It's not going to be Flicka," chanted Howard.

"Maybe she *might* be gentled," said Ken; and although his lips trembled, there was fanatical determination in his eye.

"Ken," said McLaughlin, "it's up to you. If you say you want her, we'll get her. But she wouldn't be the first of that line to die rather than give in. They're beautiful and they're fast, but let me tell you this, young man, they're *loco!*"

Ken flinched under his father's direct glance.

"If I go after her again, I'll not give up *whatever comes*, understand what I mean by that?"

"Yes."

"What do you say?"

"I want her."

"That's settled then," and suddenly Rob seemed calm and indifferent. "We'll bring her in again tomorrow or next day – I've got other work for this afternoon."

Chapter Fifteen

Ken lay face down on the pine needles under the trees on the Hill over the Green. His chin was propped in his hands. Looking down, he could see the Green and the house. Now and then he could hear voices from the kitchen. Howard was in there with their mother – he was telling her about what had happened when they brought Flicka in.

They were getting dinner. It wouldn't be long before it was time to eat. He wished he didn't have to go down at all. Howard would watch him. His father would ignore him or glare at him. And if he looked at his mother, that would be the worst of all –

The dogs were both on the terrace. It was a hot, sultry day, and Tim and Gus were putting the awning up over the Pergola. Nell had been saying for several days it was time to put it up – the sun was getting too strong. Ken watched them working at it, Tim up on the roof, Gus on

124

the terrace, pulling it and straightening it over the lattice, Tim nailing it on. Ken couldn't figure out what was going to happen. Was he going to get the filly? She was his. No one had questioned that – but would they be able to get her? Would there perhaps be several more efforts like this morning's, and then would they give up, and would his filly be forever out there on the range? Wild, alone, free – not friends with him at all? And his father not friends either? Everything a mess – the summer spoiled – Howard with Highboy, crowing over him more than ever?

There was the sound of a car coming, and looking off between the trees, Ken saw a long grey smart-looking car coming around the bend of the road. It tooled along, over the bridge, finally across the cattle-guard and up behind the house.

He wondered who it was. His father was already coming out of the front door on to the terrace, and now, around the end of the house, the visitor appeared – Ken couldn't make out who, a very tall man (not a rancher) with a wide felt hat; and his father held out both hands and gave him a loud and noisy welcome. Perhaps it was an officer from the Army Post.

Nell came running out of the house with her apron on, and there were very jolly greetings again, and then Howard came and Ken could see him introduced and shaking hands.

They talked for a while, then pulled up chairs on the terrace and sat down. His mother went back into the house. Gus and Tim had finished putting up the canvas, and went away towards the bunk house. Howard sat on the terrace wall, close enough to hear what they were saying, and played with the dogs.

Ken felt very out of it all – He wondered if the stranger was going to stay to dinner, then forgot him again thinking about Flicka. He put his head down on his arm. There was a fly somewhere near, one of the summer 'racing' flies. They raced and raced around you in circles – never went very far away. They were always there underneath the pines. Though they weren't really nice, the sound of them made you happy because they went with summer, and hot sun, and pine needles.

He poked with a stick at the pine needles, digging a little hole. There were some ants running in and out of the needles, very busy. He put his stick in the way of an ant, and watched the ant crawl over. Then he shook it off, put the stick down again, and again the ant crawled over. He could keep on doing that all morning, he thought, and a hundred times the ant would crawl over the stick and still not be getting anywhere.

Flicka – how was *she* feeling? Would she remember them? Would she hate them all, himself too? People always said horses never forgot. She had a lot of bad things to remember – Banner chasing her, and biting her; then being driven into the corral, and the way she got hurt and scratched when she crawled out.

The bell was ringing. He roused himself and looked down. Nell had sent Howard to the spring house to ring the big locomotive bell which hung in an iron frame on the very top of the peaked roof of the spring house. His father had bought the bell from the Railroad – it was bright brass and lined with scarlet, and a wire was attached to it, which hung down over the roof to the ground. There was a little wooden handle on the end of the wire. You could ring the bell by holding the wooden handle, getting a good swing going with your arms, and pulling rhythmically, and when the bell got going it sounded all over the ranch, up at the stables and down in the meadows.

Howard was ringing for him. They didn't know where he was. Ken got up, ran down the hill, crossed the Green, and went in through the kitchen so he could wash his hands and slick his hair down.

His mother was there and she seemed a little excited.

"Mr. Sargent is here, dear, he's going to stay for dinner, and we're eating in the dining room – you boys will help me –"

In a moment Ken was on the terrace shaking hands with Charley Sargent, and his father's arm was across his shoulder and he was saying, "And here's the other one – I've got a couple of jockeys, you see –"

And Charley Sargent, whom he remembered now, was shaking hands with him warmly, and he was looking up into the long, humorous face under the big sombrero; and suddenly he felt much better, because everyone seemed to have forgotten about Flicka, or that he was in disgrace again.

They had a fricassee of some cottontails he and Howard had shot yesterday evening, and his mother had cooked them with a border of fluffy white rice, and a sauce of mushrooms and cream, and Charley Sargent kept raving about the bread and asking for more and more of it, and saying he never got anything but bakery bread at home, and had thought bread baking was a lost art in Wyoming.

Howard and Ken didn't say very much, but the three grown-ups talked; and it was very interesting, because everything Charley Sargent said, he said in a funny way that made them laugh. They were talking about something very exciting – the shipping of a carload of horses from Sargent's ranch down to Los Angeles, for a man there to sell on assignment to a polo club. There was space enough in the car for four more horses, and Sargent wanted to know if McLaughlin wanted to go in with him on the deal, pay part of the shipping expenses and ship four horses.

Ken looked at his father and could see that he was in the best humour – his eyes blue and flashing, and his big white teeth laughing in his dark face; and his mother was happy too, her hair brushed so smooth and sleek down over her forehead, and her eyes, that were the same colour as the dark purple iris in the bowl on the centre of the table, wide open and smiling – and dimples in her cheeks – and she had a funny, gay remark to make to everything Charley

127

Sargent said; so, soon they were all shouting, the boys laughing too.

After dinner McLaughlin took Sargent in to his study, and Ken and Howard cleared the table while their mother washed the dishes and tidied up the kitchen, and it was while they were doing that, that they heard their father talking about Rocket.

The men were sitting with tall glasses and a bottle of Scotch, and McLaughlin was shouting.

"I'm telling you! With all your race horses, you've got nothing like this. A bronc, unbroken – nobody's been able to break her, but I can show you that she-devil running like nothing you've ever seen – twenty-five – twenty-eight – thirty miles an hour –"

Ken carried a tray of plates in to his mother, and said to her, "Dad's telling him about Rocket –"

Nell went to the door and stood listening a moment, her dish towel over her shoulder and a dripping glass in her hand. Rob and Sargent were both laughing and shouting now – "You're crazy –"

"I'm telling you! "

"There ain't no such animal! "

"What'll you bet?"

"If I could get a mare that could do twenty-eight without training –"

"If you can break her she'll make a fortune for you on the track."

"I've got a bronco-buster can break any horse that was ever foaled."

"Except Rocket! But if you can't break her, you can get race horses out of her –"

"Jake can break her, I tell you – if she's worth breaking –"

"Worth it! Didn't I tell you?"

"Can she really do thirty an hour?"

"I'll sell her to you cheap."

"How much?"

"How fast did you say?"

"Five hundred I'm asking –"

"Got a stop watch?"

"I've got a speedometer –"

Everything was forgotten except running Rocket and timing her, and before Nell had finished going over the dining-room rug with the carpet sweeper McLaughlin was out shouting for Ross and Gus, and they were all up at the stables saddling up to bring in the brood mares.

"Bring 'em all –" said McLaughlin. "I won't take the chance of bringing her in alone – I need Banner to help me."

Sargent, in his smart tweed business suit, and his tan oxfords, and a big sombrero on his thin grey hair, rode Shorty; as luck would have it the brood mare bunch were not very far away on the Saddle Back, and before the afternoon was half over, they were all in the corrals, milling around, Banner very curious as to why they were in, keeping his eye on McLaughlin. Rocket was wild-eyed and jumpy as usual, especially when she found herself singled out, separated from the others, and all alone in the small corral.

"Why the necklace?" said Sargent. "Is that a mark of special distinction?" But while he spoke, he was walking around the mare, eyeing her shrewdly, noticing the great width of chest, the wide flaring nostrils, the long, springy hocks – she was a little too high in the haunches and too long in the body. He didn't like her eyes or the way she held her nose up.

Rob was ashamed of the old piece of rope around her neck. "I've been intending to get that off her –"

"Now's a good time –"

Rob laughed. "I've told you she's a hellion. I'm likely to lose my life trying to get that rope off – I'd rather sell her first –"

McLaughlin decided to run Rocket in the Stable Pasture, along the strip of level grass just inside the fence of the County Road. He went down to the house and everyone got into the big Studebaker, Nell and the boys in the back, and Sargent beside Rob in front. They drove back up to the stables, and Ken got out and opened the gate into the Stable Pasture, the car waited for him until he had closed it, and he hopped in again. Gus was waiting inside the corral, and when McLaughlin called to him to let Rocket out, he opened the gate, and the big mare walked slowly out alone, and stood looking around, as if wondering why the others were not coming too.

McLaughlin had stopped the car. Now he started it heading for Rocket. She moved off in the right direction; the Studebaker followed; she broke into a trot, and her head came up, and her ears pricked with excitement. McLaughlin's foot pressed heavier on the throttle; the mare gave no sign of making increased effort but kept her distance easily.

Suddenly she shied out to the side; McLaughlin swerved and circled, to drive her back to the fence, but she had another idea in her head. She shot off to the woods with such speed that in a moment or two she disappeared from sight.

McLaughlin cursed freely, but followed, dodging in and out the trees, and finally taking one of the little trails that led down to Deercreek. They caught sight of the mare again as the car forded a shallow place in the stream. She was emerging from the aspens on the other side, and soon, on the hillside, came up against the fence which was the northern boundary of the pasture. She turned and trotted along beside it.

McLaughlin, noticing the way she kept hesitating, and looking over the fence, said, "She's thinking about Castle Rock Meadow again—"

The mare came to a pause and McLaughlin stopped the car, watching her.

Suddenly the mare lifted her forefeet, and without taking the trouble to jump, crashed through the fence,

130

tearing the wires, plunging on in spite of the barbs caught in her hide. In a moment she had disappeared in the woods on the other side.

At such a time McLaughlin drew on the store of profanity accumulated during his years of service in the U.S. Army.

Charley Sargent was laughing.

"She's on her way back to Castle Rock Meadow," said Rob. "She lost a colt there a couple of weeks ago, and can't get it out of her head. She'll go through every fence, the bitch. More work for Gus or me tomorrow. Here Howard, get out and mend that wire –"

He pulled a pair of pliers and wire cutters from the pocket of the car and handed them to Howard.

The boy jumped out, hunted around the fence posts until he found a loose piece of wire, cut it to the needed length, drew up the broken ends and fastened them together with the short piece.

"Now," said Rob, "we'll surprise her by meeting her at the aspen grove. She'll be there ahead of us. Hold tight, everybody!"

They bumped through the woods, following narrow paths that bored through what seemed impenetrable greenery, growing lush and thick down here by the stream. They twisted around tree trunks and stones, finally emerging from the woods on an open hillside covered with low scrub and sage, and ran along this at so tilted an angle that the car seemed about to turn over.

But when they finally reached the aspen grove, Rocket had made her investigations, and put the matter from her mind. She was grazing calmly on the range above the meadow; she had gone through or over three fences to get there.

McLaughlin was elated. "She's not far from the road that leads home over the north range. It's the flattest ground anywhere around. If she decides to go back to the corrals she's likely to take that way."

He circled up slowly behind the mare. She paid no attention. He tooted the horn. Rocket hated the horn; she looked nervously around for a moment, then headed for home with the car behind her.

It was perfect ground for a workout. No one in the car spoke now, they were intent on watching the mare. She had at last broken into a canter. Every reach took her much farther than the reach of most horses, but the astonishing thing about her was the complete lack of effort. She seemed to float along. Ken remembered, with such inner rapture that it almost choked him, that Flicka had the same effortless floating gallop. Where was this hidden power in them? Perhaps the too high haunches – the slight extra length of body.

Ken and Howard and Nell were all hanging over the back of the front seat.

"Great guns!" muttered Sargent. "She's like a locomotive – does she always run with her nose up in the air like that?"

"Yes," said Rob, "Star-gazer – "

"Get going," said Sargent. "She's not half trying."

"Look at the speedometer," said Rob.

"Jumping Jehoshaphat!" said Sargent.

The car went faster, the speedometer touched thirty. The mare appeared to be trying no harder, but kept her distance easily.

When Rocket reached the road which led in from the highway, she turned going towards the house, McLaughlin after her.

"One more burst of speed, now," cried Charley Sargent. "If that speedometer goes over thirty I'll buy her!"

"Without even trying!" scoffed Rob, pressing his foot on the throttle, and hitting the horn. At the sound of the horn, the mare bounded forward. Sargent kept one eye on the mare and one on the speedometer. It was climbing – thirty – thirty-one – thirty-three – and was wavering just short of thirty-five – as she thundered over the little stone bridge and started up the last stretch towards the Green.

"The cattle guard, Dad!" yelled Howard.

McLaughlin did not abate his speed. Nor did Rocket. When she came to the cattle guard her reach was longer, her body rose higher, but still apparently without effort, she floated over the fifteen-foot broad jump as if it had been the creek.

Rob and Sargent went to have some more drinks, and an hour later the bargain was concluded – he would buy Rocket for five hundred dollars; delivered at his ranch, sound in wind and limb.

"And just how you'll do *that*, me lad," he said grinning, "is anybody's guess."

"Leave it to me," said Rob boastfully.

Also, Rob would complete the breaking and training of the four three-year-olds, and have them ready to ship in ten days to Los Angeles in Sargent's carload of green polo horses. And so the profitable and exciting afternoon ended, and Sargent drove away.

At supper every incident of the day was talked over, even the cottontail fricassee, and Nell's bread, and how pretty the table looked with the purple iris in the centre bowl, and the way Charley Sargent looked at Nell and paid her compliments and kidded Rob.

After supper the boys went out with their twenty-twos to get more cottontails, and Rob and Nell sat on the terrace and enjoyed the evening.

There was a magical clear light over the world that seemed to emanate from the soft indigo of the sky. Right over the Hill opposite the Green was one golden star. It twinkled coquettishly, and not very far off in the sky a single, coiled mass of white cloud winked back. The cloud was full of lightning, and went on and off like an electric light. For as long as ten seconds it would flash into illumination, filled through and through with rose and gold light, then would blink a few times and go out, rumbling softly. The star twinkled merrily back. Nothing else in all the

133

twilight world moved; it was as if everything watched the little play between the star and the cloud.

At last the sky was crowded with stars, and the cloud, grumbling and flashing intermittently, moved off and disappeared behind the hills.

"The boys went down to the meadow, didn't they? Castle Rock Meadow?" asked Nell.

"Yes – went down to get some more cottontails."

Nell said nothing. A little breeze had sprung up and played through the pines on the Hill with a sound that was like a sigh. The earth and the pines seemed very black under the starlit heavens. In the darkness between twilight and moonrise, with the boys not returned from Castle Rock Meadow, Nell and Rob were uneasy and found nothing to say.

They were both glad when two dark shadows appeared on the Green and Howard's voice said, "Rocket's colt's been mauled again, there's not a speck of flesh left now – it hardly even smells."

"Maybe the mountain lion was back at it again," said Ken.

"We hunted around for tracks, before it got dark, but we didn't see any."

"What about cottontails?" asked Rob. "I thought you went out hunting."

The boys each held up two.

"Well – get on up to the spring house and skin 'em and clean 'em – it's about bedtime –"

The boys disappeared in the direction of the spring house, and presently Rob said, "Nell –"

There was no answer. He leaned over to look at her and saw that her head had fallen sideways as she sat reclining in the long canvas chair. She was sound asleep.

Chapter Sixteen

Rob had his work cut out for him next day. Banner and the mares had been driven out soon after Sargent left. Rocket, uneasy and restless in spite of a good measure of oats poured into a feed box and set on the ground, was kept alone in one of the corrals.

"The noose?" said Nell at breakfast, pouring cream in her coffee. "Are you going to bother to take that off before you load her?"

Rob looked outraged. "Do you think I would deliver her with that old string around her neck?"

Howard and Ken looked at each other. That meant getting Rocket in the chute. Rocket was to be got into the chute, then she was to be got into the truck!

"Who'll drive the truck?" asked Nell.

"I'll drive it myself. I'll take Gus along — might need him."

Breakfast was eaten quickly. McLaughlin hurried up to the corrals. Gus was told to fill the truck with petrol and oil and get it ready for the trip, Tim was to help in the chute.

They moved Rocket through the corrals without much trouble, but when she was once more in the small coop which led to the chute, and the heavy gate closed behind her, she began to snort and rear.

The narrow passage into the chute was open before her, but even though they urged her, and yelled at her, and flapped blankets and quirts over the fence on her back, she was too wise to go in. She could see through and at the far end, a heavy door blocked escape.

"It's that door," said McLaughlin. "She sees that there's no way out through the chute. We'll have to open that door, and let her see daylight through. Then perhaps if I rush her from here, I can drive her through. Ken, you get up there on top of the chute wall, close by the door. Open the door. If she rushes in, you slam the door shut. It's going to take quick thinking and quick action. You can lean down and handle the door from the top – it's not easy – mind you don't fall down into the chute. The door swings from inside out – if you get it three-quarters shut and she crashes against it, she'll shut it the rest of the way herself."

Ken climbed up on the wall of the chute, unsteady with excitement. McLaughlin, blanket on arm, climbed a few bars of the fence of the coop.

"Ready, Ken? Open the door."

Ken leaned over and hauled the door open, and at the same moment Rob gave a yell and flapped the blanket on Rocket's haunches. Rocket saw the daylight at the far end of the chute and plunged through. Ken closed the door again – just in time – the mare crashed against it.

She was right under him, and as he pulled back, she reared and her great head and wild eyes were in his face.

"Pole, Tim!" shouted McLaughlin, and Tim, standing ready, thrust through both walls of the chute a heavy pole to cut off her backward escape. It was at the height of the mare's haunches, too high for her to get her feet over, and not so high that she could back under it.

When she came down on all four feet again, and felt the pole behind her, she began to fight.

McLaughlin climbed the wall of the chute, opposite Ken, and struggled to get hold of the frantic creature's head. She reared again, and this gave him a chance to grasp the rope with both hands. She shook her head and tried to tear loose. He hung on and was almost dragged over the wall. She screamed, thrust out her head with teeth bared. McLaughlin ducked and she dropped again, breaking his hold. She put her head down on the ground and kicked. Her legs struck the wall of the chute and one got over the pole; but in the wild fury of plunges which this caused, she got it free.

Then she reared again, and McLaughlin had another chance at her head. Ken watched the look of hot anger combined with implacable determination on his father's face. He had the clippers in his right hand, waiting his chance.

Suddenly Rocket dropped to the earth and stood quiet a moment, her sides heaving with breaths that were almost groans; and McLaughlin reached his hand down, clipped the rope, and it fell free. But at that instant the mare reared sharply again, McLaughlin could not draw back quickly enough, and the top of her head struck him in the face.

Ken saw the blood spurt from his father's eye as Rocket's foam-flecked head described a complete backward arc, and she crashed to the ground, breaking the pole behind her.

For a moment McLaughlin clung to the wall, swearing, one hand to his face, while the mare fought madly below him, her feet thundering on the walls, her great body flinging itself from one side to the other.

McLaughlin got down and put his bandana to his

bleeding face. One eye was swelling rapidly. "That's that," he said, going around into the corrals.

Rocket, screaming and grunting, was struggling desperately to right herself. She had fallen so far backward that her head and neck were almost in the coop. This gave her forelegs more freedom, and by vigorous writhings and twistings, pushing and kicking with her legs, she forced herself out of the chute and into the coop, and immediately scrambled to her feet.

"We're all set now, Gus," said McLaughlin. "Bring the truck in there, back it up against the far end of the chute. Tim, you get the runway and set it in the chute. We'll drive her right through the chute up the runway and into the truck."

"Better fix dot eye, Boss," said Gus, looking at Rob's face, "und de cheek – dot's bad cut – split wide open. Let Missus fix up for you."

Rob held the handkerchief over his eye. He looked down at himself. He was spattered with foam and blood. He frowned.

"Yes, I'll go down and clean up. Gus, I don't want any more trouble with that mare. You never can tell what she'll do. Once she's in the truck, we're pretty safe, but to get her there is the trick. Better saddle Shorty. I'll ride him through the chute and up the runway, and there's a chance she might follow him into the truck."

While Tim and Gus manoeuvred the truck until its back was flush against the door of the chute, Rob went down for first aid.

"I think it really needs stitches, Rob," said Nell, examining it closely, having washed her hands in hot water and soap, and laid out all her first-aid kit on the kitchen table. "It's on the cheekbone, below the eye, really a wide cut."

"Deep?" asked Rob.

"Not so very deep."

"Fix it with tape then."

Nell held the lips of the wound closed until the bleeding had nearly stopped, then made little bridges of narrow adhesive tape across, and finally a dressing over all.

Then she put both arms around his neck and laid her cheek against his, holding him closely. He felt a slight tremor through all her body.

"Don't worry, honey," he said. "It's nothing." He patted her on the shoulder – suddenly his arms held her hard and he kissed her, then he went upstairs to change into spotless whipcord riding breeches, polished boots, and tailored jacket.

Back up at the corral again, the loading was accomplished with comparative ease. Shorty was ridden up the incline into the truck, Rocket followed. Shorty was ridden down again, and before Rocket could follow, the back of the truck was closed and escape was shut off. She was neatly enclosed in the six-foot walls of the truck, made of sturdy two-by-fours bolted together. She reared, she clawed at the rails, she neighed wildly, she plunged and leaped until again and again her feet slid out from under her and she crashed to the floor, then scrambled up to begin all over. But there was nothing she could do. No one paid any attention to her any more. Rob picked the old piece of lariat triumphantly out of the chute, and draped it around his own neck. He and Gus got into the box of the truck, and the boys begged to ride along as far as the turn on to the highway.

They passed the house, the boys hanging on the steps of the truck, shouting good-bye to Nell who came out to wave to them.

But Rocket's story was not yet ended. Where the ranch road turned off from the Lincoln Highway, was the sign of the ranch. Every rancher is proud of his ranch sign, under which all visiting cars must pass, and exercises great ingenuity in thinking up something striking and effective.

McLaughlin's sign was a high square arch. On the broad horizontal board which was the span of it, he had painted

GOOSE BAR RANCH, in red letters against a blue ground. To each side were reproductions of his brands.

As they reached the sign, Rocket's wild eyes were upon it – this strange bar, bearing down upon her from the skies – and she reared to meet it.

Standing astretch on her hind legs, her head up the sign caught her a blow on the top of the brow. There was a great crash in the truck; McLaughlin glanced back anxiously; he pulled up, and they got out and climbed up over the sides; but Rocket lay motionless. Rob got into the truck, against Gus's anxious warnings, but there was no danger, for Rocket never moved again.

The men stood about the truck, not daring to speak until McLaughlin made a move. The colour was flooding up into his face all round the swollen purple part, and there was the look of blazing fury in his eyes which Ken expected. To be baulked or beaten – to lose something he prized – this always put McLaughlin into a rage.

He laughed harshly. "Well, there we are," he shouted. "I'm glad of it. No more trouble with *that* God-damned old bitch – wish I'd shot her and all the rest of her tribe years ago – Gus, take the truck up to the old mine and dump her in – I'll walk home."

Another truck was turning in off the highway. It came abreast of them and drew up – Williams, come back, as he had said he would, for a load of cheap horses.

"I'll sell you a carcass!" McLaughlin joshed, as Williams climbed out of his truck. They explained what had happened. Williams climbed up the side of McLaughlin's truck and looked in.

"God! What a piece of luck," he said. "A fine, big mare – But I've seen things like that happen before – a little bit of a blow can kill a horse, provided you land it on the right place –"

"I've got a load of horses for you, Williams," said McLaughlin with a strange look in his eyes. "A bunch of broncs –"

"Bring 'em on," said Williams, jocularly, "if we can load 'em, I'll buy 'em –"

"All the kith and kin of this mare," said McLaughlin, savagely.

"Ought to be some good horse-flesh, if they're anything like her. How many?"

"Hardly know myself. They're all over the range. We'll have a time rounding 'em all up."

"I've got all day."

"I'll send Tim back to help you, Gus," said McLaughlin, and rode back to the ranch in Williams's truck.

When Tim came, he and Howard and Ken rode up to the old mine with Gus to see the last of Rocket.

The boys lay on the ground at the edge of the deep shaft, their faces hanging over, while the men backed the truck close to the hole, fastened ropes to Rocket's hoofs, passed them around a tree opposite, and with this leverage were able to drag the carcass to the very edge of the open back of the truck.

They removed the ropes, got in the truck, and using poles as levers, shoved and pushed at the inert black mass. She moved slightly – she was sliding – suddenly she was over.

The boys saw the great body plunge, caroming from side to side, the hoofs turn up, the mane and tail whipping and winding – then the darkness swallowed her. Nothing – and a long silence before the jarring thud three hundred feet below, that shook the earth they were lying on.

Sitting at dinner in the kitchen Williams said, "If I may be so bold, why do you wear the piece of lariat around your neck, Captain? Someone been roping *you* –"

Everyone laughed but Nell. Her face coloured up – she reached over and pulled the rope from Rob's neck, went to the stove, and lifting a lid off, dropped it into the fire.

The rest of the day was spent rounding up horses of all ages, descendants of the Albino.

At first no one had believed that McLaughlin really

meant what he said — that every single one of the Albino's blood, no matter how beautiful, how fast, or how promising, was to be sold. But as the hours went on, and one after the other was gathered into the corrals, and still they went out on horseback to gather more, with Nell busy with the stud book and names, it became apparent that he was in earnest.

Ken and Howard were kept at the gates, opening and shutting them as the different bands were brought through, taken down to the corrals, the one bronc picked out and held, the others sent out again. Gus and Tim and Ross were all riding.

"And that's every last one of them," said Nell at length, closing the book. Her voice was regretful.

She and Williams were in the stable, looking out into the corrals, over the top of the Dutch door. The two boys were perched safely on the corral fence, Rob and the men in the corral with the milling broncs.

"Except Flicka," murmured Ken, and he looked across the corral at his mother and caught her eye. She was looking at him too, thinking he knew, the same thing. He had not been exactly worried about Flicka. After all, she was his own, his father had given her to him, she couldn't be sold without his consent.

"Nine of them," said McLaughlin, counting, and Williams went out of the stable into the corral.

Now began a long period of bargaining. With the horses under their eyes McLaughlin and Williams argued until the watchers were tired.

"I could get ten in the truck," said Williams. "Haven't you got another to throw in?"

"I might have," said McLaughlin, "but let's settle the price of these first."

They did some figuring on bits of paper, and finally the deal was closed.

McLaughlin walked over to Ken, called him down from the fence, and walked away with him.

"Ken," he said quietly, "I'm going to give you a chance to do a sensible, manly thing. I want you to choose another colt, and let me sell Flicka to Williams with the rest of this hell's brew."

A wave of heat rushed all over Ken's body. He looked down, dug with his toe in the gravel of the path, and shook his head.

McLaughlin was quiet and persuasive. "You've seen for yourself – what can you expect? It's for your own sake I'm asking, as well as to save myself the trouble and un-pleasantness of trying to help you do something which is impossible. What's the use of having another Rocket on our hands? You've seen what end she came to – and no one could have tried harder with a horse than I tried with her –"

"But I'm going to *tame* Flicka," whispered Ken. "Sometimes bad horses get tamed."

McLaughlin's voice rose angrily. "Look up!"

Ken looked up and was more frightened than ever. His father's face looked appalling. It was swollen out of all shape, one eye was closed by purple and black lumps above and below, and the white dressing on the cheekbone was surrounded by an inflamed, angry circle.

"Are you going to be a bull-headed little simp or a sen-sible boy?"

Ken said stubbornly, "Dad, I have to have her – she's mine."

He really meant, *she's me*. It felt as if his father were asking him to be torn apart.

"For me, Ken, then; and for your mother – let's have a pleasant summer. Let's have *something* turn out right –"

Ken shook his head, and suddenly felt his father's hand on his shoulder, gripping with such strength it hurt him.

"I'd like to shake the teeth out of your stubborn head –" said McLaughlin savagely; then turned around and strode back to the stable. Ken followed, his heart pounding, but triumph singing within him. Flicka was his. She couldn't be taken.

"That's all," shouted McLaughlin. "Nine of them. Now we'll load 'em."

With the assistance of Shorty, the broncs were driven through the chute into the truck and penned in.

The truck stopped at the house, while Williams made out a cheque to Rob. Though it wasn't as much of a cheque as he would have got for Rocket, yet it was big enough to bring a little satisfaction into his one open eye.

"Want to ride out to the highway in the car?" Rob asked Nell. "And see the last of them?"

They all got into the Studebaker, and followed Williams along the road, watching the struggles of the horses in the truck. Although they were tightly packed, several of them, frantic with fear, were being troublesome.

One of them kept rearing, and got his forefeet over one side. The truck tilted going along the side of the hill, and suddenly the impossible happened. The bronc clawed up the side to a hold, got his body across it, and toppled over.

It was a tremendous fall, as the hill sloped down forty feet or so, and the bronc went bounding, rolling, somersaulting to the bottom.

Rob brought the Studebaker to a stop. They all jumped out and stood watching, while Williams halted his truck and got down from the box.

When the bronc hit the bottom of the hill, he leaped to his feet and stood, apparently unhurt, looking around in a comical surprised fashion. Everyone began to laugh.

Williams came back to McLaughlin. "It'll make me too late if I go back and load him again."

Rob took his cheque out of his pocket. "Here's my fountain pen – make me out a new cheque – take the price of him off –"

Williams hastened to do so as he knew that, once the broncs had been loaded in his truck, and his cheque given, the loss should have been his and not McLaughlin's. He

144

said jocularly as they exchanged cheques, "I'll let you feed him for a year and I'll buy him from you on my trip next summer."

McLaughlin said, "On your way! You want to get to the border before dark, and by the way – drive *around* the sign out there by the highway – *not under*!"

"You bet. Well – so long." Williams climbed into his truck and drove away.

The bronc was running about the meadow, looking around in an odd startled fashion as if he didn't know where he was. Suddenly he began to gallop hard, then his head went down, he turned head over heels, lay still a moment, got up and again began to gallop.

The boys looked at their father trying to read in his face the explanation of this strange behaviour. The bronc was certainly acting in an unnatural manner. Nell knew, with a sick feeling in her heart, that the beautiful young thing was injured.

McLaughlin's face was set and hard, his eyes narrowed. They stood in silence watching the colt going through the strange gyration over and over, galloping, turning head over heels, lying still a moment, then getting up and galloping again.

At last, McLaughlin said, "Is the Winchester in the car?"

"Yes," said Howard promptly. "You put it in the back when we went to look for the wildcat, remember? And told us to leave it there."

"Get it."

McLaughlin took the gun, then said, "Nell, you go on home with the boys."

"Oh, can't we stay?" said Howard.

"No. Bad enough to have to shoot him. This isn't a show."

Nell drove away with the boys, and McLaughlin took a careful position on level ground and raised the gun to his shoulder.

He wanted to be sure –

There was a long wait, until the colt came to a pause in his gambols. When at last he did, standing in the same comical, surprised fashion, as if asking what was going to happen, there was the sharp crack of the Winchester. The bullet whined, the echoes came thundering back softly from the hills, and the colt went gently down in the deep grass of the meadow.

"And that's the last of them," said McLaughlin, as he lowered the rifle and stood a moment watching, to see if there was any movement in the grass. Then he ejected the empty shell and added savagely, "*Except Flicka.*"

Chapter Seventeen

Several days passed before McLaughlin found time to make another effort to bring Flicka in, days in which he seemed to care nothing about what had happened or was going to happen. He was concerned only with his work. He drove the men hard, and Nell, too, had all she could do working with Rumba as well as attending to her housework. He ignored Ken.

The four three-year-olds were coming along nicely. The daily routine of oats, grooming, exercising, filled out their muscles and put a fine sheen on their coats. They had reached the point where they pricked their ears and pranced gaily when their trainers whistled them into the corral in the morning. Gangway had stopped his bucking, and McLaughlin put the four of them through a daily workout down in the practice field, which included the swinging of polo sticks and whacking at the ball.

On Sunday the family went to church in Cheyenne. There was the usual argument before going. Rob, who wanted to spend the morning sitting on the terrace reading the funny papers, said he thought they ought not to go because some officers might come out from the Post. "There's always a chance, you know, that someone might buy a pony."

"Not Sunday morning," said Nell firmly. And then she added with the one deep dimple in her right cheek showing, "But you don't have to go, dear, your face isn't healed up yet. That's a good excuse. I'll go and take the boys."

McLaughlin said, "Right-o." Fifteen minutes later, when Nell was ready to go and Howard and Ken were dressed in their long grey flannel trousers and white shirts and small round white linen hats with narrow brims, he came running upstairs and roared indignantly, "Do you think I'll let you go to town and sit in that pew without me by your side?"

As they waited for him to dress, the boys fidgeting, Nell explained to them that Army Officers are trained to be very particular how they look for the sake of their prestige, so they must all wait patiently.

At last McLaughlin came down looking clean and handsome in his light grey flannel suit, with a soft felt hat tilted at just the right angle on his black hair and nothing but a small piece of adhesive on his cheek bone.

Nell was in a dark green print, with turban and high-heeled pumps. Tim had washed the car, and the maroon paint and shining nickel was as bright as anything they passed on the Lincoln Highway.

McLaughlin's habitual pace was sixty-five miles an hour. Today, with a slight feeling of pressure in him, he edged it up to seventy, but as usual they were late, and made a commotion as they were ushered up the aisle of the church, with everyone seated listening to the first lesson being read.

They dined in town, with the Bartletts; and by the time they got back to the ranch, a number of visitors were there;

and from then on the pleasant sociabilities of Sunday afternoon kept the place alive with cars coming and going, trays of bottles and glasses being carried in and out, and much talk and laughter.

Children love to hear the conversation of their elders, and Howard and Ken stuck close to their father and mother, and the group of officers and officers' wives; and listened to the story of Rocket's violent death told again and again; the loco bunch described; and the Albino's prepotency and intractability discussed and commented upon.

Loco was a word Ken had heard ever since he was born. *You're loco* meant the same as, *You're crazy!* or *what a goof!* But the way it was being talked about now was different, very serious somehow . . . he didn't get it. . . .

He sat on the low stone wall of the terrace, his legs dangling over the flower border, and watched a big bumble bee boring into a purple petunia blossom, while his elders gossiped.

Gus and Ross and Tim had been talking about loco animals too.

Last night Howard and Ken had spent an hour in the bunk house before bedtime, as they often did, listening to the men swap yarns, and the talk was all about what made animals loco in the first place.

Tim told a tale of a little black colt who was chased by a pack of coyotes; the mother defended it bravely. But all through the night the mare and the foal were in terror of their lives. They fought and ran, and turned to fight again. And by the morning the colt's hair had turned pure white, and it was loco.

The bronco-buster had a story to match that.

He'd been talking about the horses he had on his own ranch. He had built up a band by catching wild mustangs, breaking them, now and then trading for a good mare. "But to tell the truth there wasn't a real good horse on the place. Them catch colts – they're hard as hell to pull in. I'd go out a-huntin' and mebbe see a bunch strung out on the sky line – ridge runners – they git up on a high place where they kin see you comin' a mile off – and like as not you never catch sight of 'em agin – if you do git a few and git 'em broke, you ain't got nuthin'.

"My top horse was one of them catch colts. He waan't no good. Cold-mouthed, couldn't feel the bit at all, just didn't savvy. I made up my mind I'd get a real good colt, bred right, and raise him to be Top Horse.

"Waall, I had a good mare and I paid ten dolars for service by a Government stud."

"Service comes free from Government studs," said Gus.

"The ten bucks was the cost of hirin' a trailer and transportin' my mare. A year later, she dropped a foal, and he grew up a beauty. Long straight legs and eyes as soft as a woman's. Smart little feller too. When he was a yearlin' I rode his mother out to a homestead I had put under fence out by Centennial, and the colt come along with us. You know that country up there? Them old cock-eyed mountains goin' straight up into the sky – and nary a house or a road or a human being as fur as you kin see. I had set my fence the summer before; but that ole wind got-a-whippin' and a-pullin' it and laid it down for half a mile. I had a week's work cut out for me. It was while I was havin' a smoke after dinner one day that I seen this big mountain lion jump the yearlin'. The yearlin' was off there a ways, a-grazin, clost to a hillside; and that cat came a-shootin' down through the air and lit on top the colt. Ever see one of them lions? Stand as high as a new born colt – an scream like a woman – enough to curdle your blood. Lie in the trees, on tops of rocks, leap on colts or horses as they go by."

"How can they kill a horse?" demanded Howard.

"It's a real neat trick. Leap up on top the neck, and bite in at the base of the spine and hang on with their front claws. The rest of 'em's a-swingin' under the horse's head and neck, with the hind feet hooked under

150

the horse's chin, clawin' agin it. The weight of the crittur twists the horse's head plumb around and breaks its neck. Down it goes and the rest is pickins."

"Did it kill your colt?"

"Nope. He screamed and went down and rolled, an' the ole lady was grazin' not so very fur away, and she come on the run and went for the cat. Cats ain't brave – don't put up much of a fight. They'd ruther run if they don't get the drop an' kill with the first leap. It took to the tall timber, and by the time I got my gun and was a-lookin' for a shot, there waan't a sign of it. But the colt could never stand no one on his back after that. When he got older, I did my best to break him, but he'd keep a-lookin' round at me, shakin', jumpin' – never did git him broke. He ended up plumb loco."

All of this talk drifted hazily through Ken's mind, while he watched the bumble bee boring its way into a half opened petunia bud. The bee was completely hidden and the weight of it bowed the blossom almost to the ground. Ken waited to see it come out again. What a world that must be to get into, the very heart of a little flower – if he was a bumble bee now—

Behind him on the terrace, the Major's wife was teasing Rob and Nell to come to a dance next Saturday night at the Post. "We never see you two in town," she said. "Not that I blame you— If I had a place like this—"

"Remember last time we went to a dance at the Post?" said Rob grinning.

"Do I!" exclaimed Nell. "Last fall. And there was a flood while we were away."

"I remember," yelled Howard. "The water was over the bridge coming back, and you couldn't drive over!"

Ken remembered too; it had been an exciting night. Just before bed-time, when he and Howard were sauntering home after a stroll with Gus, there had been a great roar, and a wave of water came down Lone Tree Creek and left a wide river in the meadow where there had only been a creek before. The dogs rushed down and barked at the water and it covered the stone bridge that led up the cattle guard, and the parapets of the bridge, too.

"There we were about four in the morning," said Rob, "driving in from the highway, and my headlights picked up water in front, where there should have been a road, and we got out to see what had happened, and there was a river between us and home."

"For mercy's sake," screamed Mrs. Gilfillan. "What did you do?"

"You should have seen us. The parapets of the bridge were only about one foot under water. So we took off our shoes and stockings, I rolled up my trousers, Nel picked up her skirts, and we waded across on the parapets – left the car where it was till morning –"

"Did you say a party at the *Post*?" kidded Lieutenant Grubb. "And anyone going home sober enough to walk a couple of tight ropes over a river –"

There was one of the jovial roars of laughter from everyone that made Howard and Ken join in without exactly understanding what the joke was.

The bumble bee came out of the petunia and circled around, tasting several flowers in succession, then found one it liked and bored in again.

Ken saw Pauly sitting over a gopher hole at the far side of the Green. She was waiting for the gopher to stick its head out. She sat as still as a little brown statue, braced on her front paws, her eyes down into the hole. She would wait there ten minutes – fifteen – twenty – and at last the gopher wouldn't be able to stand it any longer and he'd stick his head out to see if she'd gone away –

They were talking about Rocket again.

Major Gifillan said, "No reason, course, why there shouldn't be inherited insanity among animals just as there is among human beings, but –"

Lieutenant Grubb interrupted. "How could you ever be sure what it is? There are all sorts of temperaments. Just sheer intractibility, or too high spirits, would give you the same type. And that's not necessarily insanity, nor is it a bad thing. Take humans – for instance, a youngster too spirited to control –"

"It *is* a bad thing," interrupted the Major. "And you might as well call it insanity, for it amounts to an inability to adjust to environment."

"But when that type *does* adjust, you've got something super."

"How many of them ever do? Most of them beat their heads against the wall until they beat their brains out."

"Even so, I maintain that it's not insane for a free-dom-loving individual man or beast, to refuse to be sub-dued."

Tim and the little bronco-buster sauntered down the Green, going to find the cows and bring them in for milk-ing.

Colonel Harris said, "My experience has been that the high-strung individual, the nervous, keyed-up type – is apt to be a fine performer. It's the solitary, or the queer fellow, that I'm afraid of. Show me a man who plays a lone hand – no natural gregariousness, you know – the *lone wolf* type – and I'll show you one who's apt to be screwy."

Pauly was still sitting motionless over the gopher hole. Suddenly she made one smooth, lightning stroke of her paw across the opening, and then she crouched, struggling with something that was alive. Her head was turned side-ways, she was crunching. Presently it wasn't alive any longer, and Pauly stood up, lifted her head with the dead gopher hanging from her jaws, and slowly trotted up the Hill into the woods.

". . . in some cases, an actual psychosis, no doubt about it," said the Major.

The words danced in Ken's brain. He didn't know what they meant, but it didn't matter. He was too happy. That morning in church, he had suddenly nudged Nell, and when she looked down into his beaming face, she realized the minister had just read the words *beautiful upon the mountains*. Ken's lips silently formed the word *Flicka*, and Nell smiled back. All week he had thought of nothing but Flicka. She got into his conversation – he would be talking about *she* this, and *she* that – and his father would suddenly roar, "What *she*?" His father was grim and angry with him, but not even that worried him.

Every night when he went to bed, he lay awake thinking of Flicka as long as he could. He would see her floating over the ravines, flattened in a leap, her long slim legs stretched forward and back until she seemed just a slightly curved line, suspended. And he would see her face as if it was close to his own. In reality he had seen her close to, only once. That was the first time when she had fled past him, terrified, and had cast him a glance. Then her face had been so close he could almost have leaned over and touched it. Some day, he thought, he would. He'd stroke her face, he'd brush out that untidy bang of hair, he'd put it neatly between her eyes, he'd put his own cheek right against her soft nose.

At odd moments, a very ecstasy of possession filled him. Now, sitting on the terrace wall, his heart sang, and he hung his head for fear everyone could see the pride and joy shining out of his eyes. . . .

Behind him they were all shouting with laughter again, and he turned to see what it was about. His mother was telling something that made them laugh. She was saying that the reason Rob had looked so rakish driving to church that morning was the way he wore his hat.

"It's the whole thing –" she said. "the way a man wears his hat. It can make him look like a – a – respectable gentleman –" (There were shouts at this) "or a rake," she went on, ("Bring him on," giggled Mr. Gilfillan) "or a pompous ass –" (The Major whacked Colonel Harris on the back and said, "Get up and bow, Colonel") "or very, *very* careful –" finished Nell, and the Lieutenant said, "I never can be good, so I'm just careful."

Then they got trying on hats in different ways.

Ken and Howard tried on hats too, strutting about; and Mrs. Gilfillan and Mrs. Grubb put on the boys' little white linen hats and sat there with them perched on their blonde heads.

Later in the afternoon, McLaughlin stuck a tin can on the tip of one of the branches of a pine tree on the Hill opposite and the officers took their revolvers and practised target shooting, standing on the terrace.

Their father told the boys to get their twenty-twos and give an exhibition of markmanship, and at last he brought out the big guns, the Express rifle, and the Winchester, and the officers all tried shooting with them, and the long shells went crashing across the valley, chipping off pieces of the cliff half a mile away, until Tim came up from the barn, his face darker and redder than usual, saying that he couldn't milk the cows, with the big guns booming over the barn – they'd kicked over two buckets already.

Then Mrs. Grubb and Mrs. Gilfillan said they wanted to ride out and see the brood mares, so they all crowded into two automobiles, and McLaughlin led the way.

When they found the brood mares, the stopped some distance off and got out, and McLaughlin promised that Banner would come out to meet them and do the honours.

"How do you know he will?" asked Mrs. Gilfillan.

"He always does."

The mares stopped grazing and stood, alert, curious, and ready to run. Banner was amongst them.

His head topped them all, and even from a distance, the men and women watching could feel the penetration of his eye.

Suddenly the big stallion moved towards them, ears pricked, inquiring eyes wide and fearless, and began to trot, his legs alternating in high, free, curving steps, his mane streaming, his tail up.

"Flying all his flags! cried Nell.

A roar and a cheer burst from the officers as the stallion,

without breaking his trot, increased his pace and came down the wind to them like a bugle call.

Banner halted ten yards off and stood looking the group over. His golden coat blazed in the sunshine.

"What an intelligent face!" exclaimed the Colonel. McLaughlin, still in his grey suit and rakish hat, went forward to the stud, apologizing gravely for not having brought a bucket of oats in the car.

Lying in bed that night, Ken remembered the way Banner had looked. Banner, the Sire of Flicka – Flicka was the same, the same burnished gold, the same beauty, the same flags flying – Oh, *mine* . . . my colt . . . my own . . . my *very* own . . .

He wondered when his father would bring her in again.

He had been wondering that every day when Gus put his round pink face in at the kitchen door and said, "What's today, Boss?" But his father had planned other work. Meadows to be taken care of, water to be turned out of one ditch and into the other. Endless hours of work on the three-year-olds that must be ready to ship in just a few days now. A new cattle guard being built at one of the railroad gates.

But next morning, when Gus said, "What's today, Boss?" McLaughlin gave the order for the day's work and then said, "And I think –" and paused.

Ken looked down to hide his excitement, he clenched his fists under the table.

McLaughlin went on, "Tomorrow we'll get the yearlings in again, Gus, and cut out Ken's filly. I want to do that before Ross leaves. We may need his help."

Tomorrow . . .

ENID BLYTON is Dragon's bestselling author. Her books have sold millions of copies throughout the world and have delighted children of many nations. Here is a list of her books available in Dragon Books:

FIRST TERM AT MALORY TOWERS	30p ☐
SECOND FORM AT MALORY TOWERS	30p ☐
THIRD YEAR AT MALORY TOWERS	30p ☐
UPPER FOURTH AT MALORY TOWERS	30p ☐
IN THE FIFTH AT MALORY TOWERS	30p ☐
LAST TERM AT MALORY TOWERS	30p ☐
MALORY TOWERS GIFT SET	£1.35 ☐
6 Books ENID BLYTON	

THE TWINS AT ST. CLARE'S	30p ☐
SUMMER TERM AT ST. CLARE'S	30p ☐
SECOND FORM AT ST. CLARE'S	30p ☐
CLAUDINE AT ST. CLARE'S	30p ☐
FIFTH FORMERS AT ST. CLARE'S	30p ☐
THE O'SULLIVAN TWINS	30p ☐
ST. CLARE'S GIFT SET	£1.35 ☐
5 Books ENID BLYTON	

MYSTERY OF THE BANSHEE TOWERS	30p ☐
MYSTERY OF THE BURNT COTTAGE	30p ☐
MYSTERY OF THE DISAPPEARING CAT	30p ☐
MYSTERY OF THE HIDDEN HOUSE	30p ☐
MYSTERY OF HOLLY LANE	30p ☐
MYSTERY OF THE INVISIBLE THIEF	30p ☐
MYSTERY OF THE MISSING MAN	30p ☐
MYSTERY OF THE MISSING NECKLACE	30p ☐
MYSTERY OF THE PANTOMIME CAT	30p ☐
MYSTERY OF THE SECRET ROOM	30p ☐
MYSTERY OF THE SPITEFUL LETTERS	30p ☐
MYSTERY OF THE STRANGE BUNDLE	30p ☐
MYSTERY OF THE STRANGE MESSAGES	30p ☐
MYSTERY OF TALLY-HO COTTAGE	30p ☐
MYSTERY OF THE VANISHED PRINCE	30p ☐

TALES FROM THE BIBLE	30p ☐
CHILDREN'S LIFE OF CHRIST	30p ☐

THE BOY WHO TURNED INTO AN ENGINE	30p ☐
THE BOOK OF NAUGHTY CHILDREN	30p ☐
A SECOND BOOK OF NAUGHTY CHILDREN	30p ☐

PONY BOOKS are very popular with boys and girls.
Dragon Books have a fine selection by the best authors to choose from:

SPECIAL DELIVERY	Gillian Baxter	17p	☐
PANTOMIME PONIES	Gillian Baxter	17p	☐
SILVER BRUMBY'S KINGDOM	Elyne Mitchell	30p	☐
SILVER BRUMBIES OF THE SOUTH			
	Elyne Mitchell	30p	☐
SILVER BRUMBY	Elyne Mitchell	30p	☐
SILVER BRUMBY'S DAUGHTER	Elyne Mitchell	30p	☐
MY FRIEND FLICKA PART 1	Mary O'Hara	30p	☐
MY FRIEND FLICKA PART 2	Mary O'Hara	30p	☐
GREEN GRASS OF WYOMING 1	Mary O'Hara	25p	☐
GREEN GRASS OF WYOMING 2	Mary O'Hara	25p	☐
GREEN GRASS OF WYOMING 3	Mary O'Hara	25p	☐
THUNDERHEAD 1	Mary O'Hara	25p	☐
THUNDERHEAD 2	Mary O'Hara	25p	☐
THUNDERHEAD 3	Mary O'Hara	25p	☐
FOR WANT OF A SADDLE			
	Christine Pullein-Thompson	30p	☐
IMPOSSIBLE HORSE	Christine Pullein-Thompson	30p	☐
THE SECOND MOUNT	Christine Pullein-Thompson	25p	☐
THE EMPTY FIELD	Christine Pullein-Thompson	25p	☐
THREE TO RIDE	Christine Pullein-Thompson	25p	☐
THE PONY DOPERS	Christine Pullein-Thompson	25p	☐
A SWISS ADVENTURE	Pat Smythe	20p	☐
A SPANISH ADVENTURE	Pat Smythe	25p	☐

All these books are available at your local bookshop or newsagent; or can be ordered direct from the publisher. Just tick the titles you want and fill in the form below.

Name...

Address ....

....

Write to Dragon Cash Sales, P.O. Box 11, Falmouth, Cornwall TR10 9EN
Please enclose remittance to the value of the cover price plus 10p postage and packing for one book, 5p for each additional copy.
Granada Publishing reserve the right to show new retail prices on covers, which may differ from those previously advertised in the text or elsewhere.